What others are saying about *A Stone for Amer*:

"Having read all three of your books (trilogy) . . . I wish to thank you for the prodigious amount of creative thought you put into this [work], all tied together in a long reflective car trip of Callie with her father, Will. . . . You have a writing gift, using words so eloquently to introduce characters who grow in size and memory and significance as you write."
> —Don Draayer, former Superintendent, Minnetonka School District 276

"I finished *A Stone for Amer* today. Loved it . . . beautiful descriptions, clear metaphors, tight dialogue. . . . I was pulled into the times of the 1950s, as well as Amer's story. . . ."
> — Jodi Anderson, Literary Coördinator, Greeley/Evans Public Schools, Colorado

"It isn't unusual for local authors to receive endorsements from fellow writers in this supportive literary community. But Szarke is earning raves from an exceptional group, including poet/oral historian and environmental writer Joe Paddock; syndicated newspaper columnist, *Minneapolis Star Tribune*, author and University of Minnesota senior fellow Stephen Wilbers; novelists Faith Sullivan and Pamela Carter Joern; and 'Minnesota Bound' TV host Ron Schara."
> —Mary Ann Grossmann, book editor for the *St. Paul Pioneer Press*

"This novel in stories [*Lady in the Moon*] is the third in the author's Callie series, following her award-winning *Delicate Armor* and *A Stone for Amer*. Like her previous books, this one is easy to read and brings to life ordinary people."
> —Mary Ann Grossmann, *St. Paul Pioneer Press*

A Stone
for Amer

"Keep on singing" JJ

A Stone
for Amer

Connie Claire Szarke

Heron Bay Publishing
Minneapolis

Heron Bay Publishing
Minneapolis

Published by Heron Bay Publishing
www.heronbaypublishing.com

This is a work of fiction based on a true story. Many names, characters, places, and incidents are the products of the author's imagination, or are used fictitiously. Some resemblance to actual events, locales, and persons, living or dead, is entirely coincidental.

ISBN: 978-0-9885363-5-7

Second Edition, April 2017
Book design, Dorie McClelland, springbookdesign.com
Printed in the United States of America

To the memory of Clair Drager Peterson,
who provided the seeds for this story.

To Leo Aran and Roman Django.

And to the memory of Matthew Shepard, 1976–1998

Also by CONNIE CLAIRE SZARKE

Lady in the Moon, A Novel in Stories, part of the Callie Lindstrom trilogy
Heron Bay Publishing, 2016

Delicate Armor, part of the Callie Lindstrom trilogy, second edition
Heron Bay Publishing, 2014

Omertà, a stand-alone short story set in Sicily
Heron Bay Publishing, 2015

Stone Wall, a short story set in Ireland,
Red Dragonfly Press, Minnesota, 2012

Contents

"Whither is fled the visionary gleam?
Where is it now, the glory and the dream?"

—William Wordsworth

Chapter 1

Know That He Mattered in This World

1986

IT FEELS GOOD to walk around this cemetery, stretch these old legs after such a trip—more like a great journey at my age. Came all the way from Minneapolis. "Minnenapolis," as my brother called it. Sure wish Ray could have come with us—my daughter Callie and me—but we haven't been in touch for so long. He might be in a nursing home for all I know. Can't seem to recall the last time I saw him.

Anyhow, it's too bad he hasn't been in on this ordeal from the beginning—the life and story of Uncle Amer. Ah, but that's water over the dam now. Or water under the bridge. Whichever way you want to look at it. Maybe some day I'll be able to tell my brother how it was for our uncle. That is, if he'll sit for it.

It's awfully hot for September. I'm too warm in my suit and tie. And sometimes my knees feel like the sound of my old garage door opening and closing. For nearly an hour we've been wandering through this ancient section of the Swedish cemetery here in Rockford, Illinois, searching for a marker—one that I've tried to visualize for some time. I must be looking a little weary, a bit tipsy, because my daughter just rushed over to grab my arm.

"You doing all right, Dad?" she asks. "Maybe we ought to take a break, go have a cup of coffee. I'm beginning to wonder if we should've bothered coming all this way."

"I can tell you right now, Cal, I'm not giving up. If I could look at my uncle lying in that dirt basement back in Montana, I sure as hell can shuffle around these headstones until I find him. We're not leaving until I do."

Callie lets go my arm, smirks, and soft-shoes her way through the grass over to the next row of stones.

I know she's glad to have made this trip with me. Good for both of us to get away from home for a couple of days; for me, to think of other things besides my health, and for my daughter, a road trip to help clear the air after dealing with past marital issues. Focusing on the life and death of her great-uncle has always served as an incremental lesson from early on up.

When she was a little girl, Cal discovered Amer's trunk in our cottage near Lake Shetek; it was filled with curious things: a shaving mug, old photographs, personal letters, and fascinating novels, including *The Picture of Dorian Gray*, published in 1891. There were also Montana newspaper articles and trial records loaded with startling information. And an unforgettable picture of my uncle's dog, Radge, standing on a trail, glancing up at the sky—looking as if something nearby had just gone free and left this earth for good.

From then on, Callie insisted on learning more about Amer. And so she grew up hearing me tell his story—that is, most of it.

I WAS SIXTEEN when my father, Victor, and I rode the train out West to claim Amer's body. Turning eighty-five next birthday.

Well, you might say, that was a long time ago. True. But I'm still bitter about how he died. For some things in life, time has no business figuring in. The way I see it, there aren't any limits. A fellow (or a woman, as Callie would have me say) can hurt just as much over an age-old wound as he would from yesterday's sorrow.

Cal and I drove the three hundred and fifty miles, in part to visit relatives—though more of them are planted in this cemetery than live in town. But mainly I'm here, after all these years, to see that my uncle's grave has been done up as it should be, set with a decent tombstone, as promised by his brothers.

Why did it take me so long to return to Rockford? My daughter and I discussed that during our road trip. While she did the driving, I talked about all the usual reasons people put off going places, making pilgrimages. The years peel by, I told her, when a fella's out there earning a living, raising a family, taking care of a home or three. That's how it was for Emily and me. There was our house in Masterton, along with my mother Julia and her house. And then there was the cottage on Lake Shetek. I was responsible for all three properties. Oh, I managed all right. Except for my brother, I had a family member help me out from time to time. Then, of course, Emily and I had our two daughters, Liz and Callie, to look after, along with my work at the Maywood County courthouse, where I served as auditor.

Travel was a luxury during the war years. After that, our decades slipped away like northern pike through a rip in my landing net.

So now, here we are.

It felt a little strange to see Hannah and Nellie when Cal and I pulled up in front of their house. Haven't seen these cousins since Mother's funeral back home in Masterton, that sad and embarrassing day when Ray and his wife ransacked our mother's house, made off with her bedding, silverware, china, and stacks of piano music. Which was particularly upsetting for Callie, because at thirteen she had already learned how to play all those notes from the sheets of "Beautiful Dreamer" and "Show Girl" and "Ain't Nature Grand?" Off they went in the trunk of my brother's car. Hell, Ray and Eloise and their daughter, Jenny, didn't even bother to join the rest of us for eats and coffee after the funeral service. I ought to be over all that by now. But nope! It's one thing still sticks in my craw.

With not much in common, these cousins and I had lost touch. Besides, I didn't care to discuss the rift between my brother and me.

Still don't. As for their dads (my other uncles), they must have set some kind of stone for Amer—maybe even a Lindstrom marker to include Grandma and Auntie. Now, if we can just find them. . . .

On our way here, Cal reminded me of my sudden decision to make this trip. Talked about what I'd said that afternoon while we were at a Leech Lake pow wow back in Minnesota. A year ago this October, we had even gone to the Hunting Moon Pow Wow, and that seemed to have started up the engine for traveling to Rockford.

"Something resonated with you that day," said Callie, driving my '85 Cadillac as if it were a racecar. "I could tell."

"Maybe so," I admitted, leaning over to glance at the speedometer. "Slack up, Cal, you're going too fast."

"I'm only doing sixty-five," she said, easing off the gas pedal—as she should.

"Well," I told her, skipping back to my reasons for not planning this trip sooner, "we didn't just hop into a car and go places in those days—our Nash, for instance. Not like today with folks ramming around all over the place, ignoring speed limits, acting as if this whole world is nothing but a racetrack. In my day, we slowed down, took the time to look around, notice nature, conserve on gas and tires. Those are still the rules, as far as I'm concerned."

"Maybe we should have walked to Rockford, huh, Dad? Like we did going to Ocheyedan. Remember Ocheyedan?"

"Unforgettable," I said, relaxing against my seatback, feeling a bit young again, loose as a sack of fresh oats. "Your mother and Liz thought we looked like a couple of vagabonds marching down that Main Street."

"Yeah," she giggled, "and when it came time to hug us, they snuffled, looking as though they needed a pair of clothespins."

"Hah, good for what ailed them."

When Cal was twelve, we strapped on backpacks and hiked from Masterton to Ocheyedan, Iowa. It took us three days to reach our destination, meandering along gravel roads, across bean fields and cornfields, around lakes, sleeping under the stars. A wonderful time, welcomed by peering deer and birdsongs along the way, with billowy clouds floating overhead. When we finally paraded into that little town, we saw Emily and Liz standing in the center of the street, next to our black Pontiac, waiting to pick us up. Of course, it was good to see them, but my heart and mind were still back there in those open stretches of wilderness, the great outdoors.

"A hell of a lot of fun, wasn't it, kiddo?"

"Damn right, Dad."

"Yup, that was some hike." I reclined my car seat and settled in for a little snooze. "Keep her below sixty, Cal. We'll get there in plenty of time."

"I'll think about it," she warbled—as usual, through a silly grin.

I was glad that my daughter could make this trip with me, not only for my sake, but for hers too. Emily and I knew it would take time for Cal to recover from the harsh treatment she had endured throughout much of her marriage. But en route to Rockford, traveling through prairie land, hazy before sunrise, I could already see that she was doing fairly well, talking about various people out of our past, and how they got through their own issues. Now I could tell that Cal was tapping into a reserve of strength and reality that her mother and I had worked to build in our two girls. Fortunately, Liz picked up on it at a young age. It took Callie a bit longer to realize that not every person in this world is kind and trustworthy.

Makes me feel better now to see that she's able to move forward on her own with a new place to live.

Which is something I have to work on now—moving forward. Truth be told, one that I'll never admit to my family, although they're likely sensing it, the main reason I decided to come back to Rockford is that, as the saying goes, I'm feeling my mortality. Emily and I won't be returning to California this winter. And I've made a mental list of things I need to do before my time is up. This road trip made the top of that list.

Throughout the years, I've never really thought about Uncle Amer packed into the ground, lying there for the rest of eternity, though I was here, at age sixteen, when he got lowered. As long as I could tell his story, he lingered for me above good old terra firma like a spirit, a shadow, in all his likeness, laboring in the fields, tending livestock— so kind to the cattle, chickens, horses, pigs—and spending the sunrise hour singing, and the moonrise hour playing his violin. I can still see him dancing through the cornrows back on our farm near Hadley, singing and romping with our dogs, like Mr. Bojangles.

Even Cal used to talk about him as if he were still alive. Heck, she was just a little girl when she discovered that big trunk full of Amer's things in the second floor storeroom of my parents' cottage at Tepeeotah: stacks of classic books, these beautifully written letters to the family, old phonograph records, court documents and legal papers sent to my father, Vic Lindstrom, Amer's brother. And then there was that picture of his dog, Radge, standing next to a trail lined with rocks, with a few trees off to one side. It had been developed in black and white, of course, then brought to life with various shades of colored ink. I'll never forget the look on that dog's face.

We brought Radge home with us from Montana. For a long time, whenever we spoke of Amer, mentioning his name, this Border Collie would stop whatever he was doing, stand perfectly still, glance at us and then gaze up at the sky with such a tender look, as if he were searching for his master in those heavens above.

If our praise could have kept him alive, that dog would have lived forever.

For the longest time, Cal held onto the paper image of Radge, and read only Amer's early letters, which I have tucked here in my suit coat pockets. She put off opening those final correspondence envelopes containing witness testimonies, articles from the *Lewistown Democrat News*, and the coroner's report. I could tell that as a youngster she wasn't ready to absorb such final and horrific pieces. She preferred to dance around as if Amer were still alive back there in Jordan, Montana. As if he were still playing *O Mio Babbino Caro* on his violin, and singing the lyrics.

Placing my hand against a pack of Amer's letters inside my breast pocket, I gazed out of the car window at a sparkling lake surrounded by fields, and let my thoughts drift back once again to that afternoon at the Leech Lake pow-wow near Federal Dam. What was it about the steady beat of that drum? From the moment we entered the gate, I felt it deep inside my chest: that constant, intense, penetrating rhythm of the drum; those powerful dancers with painted faces, flamingly colored costumes, fiery feathers; the elders who wore long, gray braids and sang those same notes, their voices starting high on the scale, descending to a lower pitch, then hovering, hovering until the birds of my mind took flight. I watched the Indians pause for another breath in order to begin again. And always, always, the beating of the drum.

What was it about that afternoon? All I know is that was the day when something told me it was time to put things to right. Wrap up any business left undone. Mend fences with my brother. Make sure Uncle Amer had been laid to rest in proper fashion, with a stone to mark his final place.

And that, you see, is what this trip is all about.

I wanted Emily and Liz to come along but they declined, eager to attend some big shindig in Masterton with the ladies from Emily's former 500 Club; all still kicking, except for Hulda Swenson. I don't know what got the better of her. My guess is that it had something to do with the long ago death of her young daughter and the fact that Doc Nelson, for some reason, never returned to check up on her bleeding after a routine tonsillectomy. I have a hunch that the pain and bitterness of losing that beautiful child took its final toll. And, as Callie used to say, "Hulda Swenson couldn't ever get another baby."

Liz and her hubby, Brian, are driving over from Wisconsin to take Emily back to our hometown for the occasion. I'd like to see my old friends and neighbors again, especially Carl Ryan and Ted Claussen. Used to hunt ducks with them at Klinker Slough, north of Lake Wilson. I might have gone along with the rest of my family, but Callie and I had already planned this road trip to Rockford.

Truth be known, I'm not so keen on going back to Masterton just yet, since the powers-that-be destroyed our stately courthouse and replaced it with some wimpy building at the head of Main Street. Just imagine! Maywood County Courthouse, built in 1891, placed on the National Register of Historic Buildings in 1977, and four years later, some gang found an excuse to tear it down. The almighty dollar most likely crowned the black heart of that deal. At least they couldn't rip out my memory of the place: the clock tower dome; the yellow brick and limestone arched portico; those stone steps worn concave; the sounds of farm boots crossing the heavy chain-and leather-linked tread inside the entry; the smells of ledgers and ink; cigarette smoke drifting up from the basement; my office on the left with its lofty, crenellated ceiling. Leading upstairs to the courtroom curved the long, ornate banister made shiny from a century of hands—smooth as the belly skin on a young bullhead. For twenty-three years, I kept the books inside that building—golden warm on the coldest of winter mornings.

Oh, I'll go back to Masterton one day, but, damn it, not until I'm good and ready.

As for our grandkids, Josie and Brent, why we hardly see them now that they're all grown up and leading busy lives—typical of young people these days. They're good kids, just not always interested in us old folks. Although, I'm pleased to say that Josie has recently paid some attention to our family history, especially Amer's. Some day, I'd like to bring her to Rockford, show her the house on State Street, where I was born. And McNeil Road, named after Mother's Uncle Abe. I'll bet she'd like to see that huge building that went up at the hands of a barn-raising crew. I was in fourth grade at the time, glad to return for a visit. And then, there was the old schoolhouse. But it's not a school any longer. Someone turned it into a house. Times change.

This time, it's just the two of us—Cal and me. Besides, as Emily made sure to mention before sending us on our way, "It's fitting for you and Callie to make this trip by yourselves."

In a way she's right. As you know, Cal has always taken a sharp interest in what happened to Uncle Amer. Grew up hearing me tell his story since she was old enough to understand most of it. The other day she asked me to set the whole thing down on paper. I'd like to oblige. In fact, I tried several times to scribble a few memories. But I'm a better talker than writer. Always have been, except with numbers, of course. Lately, though, when I get to the end, there seems to be something missing. I told my family I need to see Amer's grave. Witness some tangible evidence. Make sure that all who pass by can read his name and know that he mattered in this world.

Here is how Cal and I picture his tombstone:

Amer Lindstrom

Born 1880 • Died 1919

Chapter 2

A Place Called God's Country

HANNAH AND NELLIE, my cousins who live in Rockford, are here in the cemetery with us. Besides my brother and me, they're the only relatives left out of that whole batch of Lindstroms. We already paid our respects in the newer section where their parents are buried under elaborate black headstones with the shapes of plows and furrows etched on them. But here, most of the fog-colored tombstones require better eyesight than I have, though who would want to admit that? It's not easy making out names and dates carved in soft, grayish white stone grown over with dark moss and yellow lichens.

During the better part of a hundred years, rain, sleet, hail, snow, wind, and a hot sun have worn the lettering to shallow troughs, leaving shadowy hints of who lies buried beneath and how old they were when felled by disease or old age or murder or heaven knows what else fate had in store for them.

Which reminds me of those two Swedish brothers back home, near Iona. Einar and Arvid, old farmers, never married, were out hunting pheasants along the cut rows of their cornfield. One shot the other; accidentally, so he said. For three more years, Einar lived on in the family farmhouse, across from their barn that had caved in like a giant swayback horse soon to go down on its knees, unable to get up again—as if it had just lost heart.

One cold winter afternoon, Einar was found dead in the living room, next to a heating drum filled with kerosene. Both brothers now lie next to their parents in the Masterton graveyard, beneath a small gray stone obelisk covered in lichens and shallow lettering, similar to what I'm seeing here in the Rockford Swedish cemetery.

No amount of squinting through my bifocals at these chalky blocks reveals complete answers. Anyhow, it turns out that most of the lettering is in Swedish.

"My, oh my!" Hannah's sharp voice startles me. "It's like trying to decipher hieroglyphs, don't you know?"

"Yah, yah," answers Nellie.

Oh, these women. How they lag behind, inching past each marker and rough gray slab as if they had all the time in the world. Can't they remember where Amer is? They should be able to lead us directly to him. After all, they come here often enough. Oh, well, they're elderly, so what can I say? Hell, I might as well just stand here for a while and look around.

The entry is impressive—a tall, ornate wrought-iron gate with the name Rockford Swedish Cemetery welded at the top; backwards now, from my vantage point. A car path circles the perimeter with two intersecting roads, like an oddly shaped pie cut into quarters.

The trees are huge in this old section. Majestic. Of course, it's no surprise that they're much taller than they were seventy years ago. But how those maple and cottonwood branches sprawl across the firmament. And how the spruce and arborvitae stand like giant sentinels, towering over the graves, waving their long arms. I may be hard of hearing, but I can still make out the shushing sound of the wind tracking through these boughs. And even though it's hot out, I can smell autumn in the air.

Suddenly, high above the ground, a gray squirrel leaps through the air from a maple branch over to the cottonwood tree. He reminds me of one that I spotted last winter near Callie's place on the lake. Searching for the easiest spot to take off from, that scrawny gray paused, jumped, and nearly fell from a two-story-high limb, dangling from the limp branch tip by his front paws for a second before collecting himself and racing through the bare branches like an Olympic gold medalist. Whew!

Cal takes my arm and rests her head against my shoulder while we pause before a cluster of infants' graves. Without saying, we remember Billy, Emily's and my baby boy who died in his crib several years before Cal was born. I wish he could have known Liz and Callie, his big and little sisters. And I wish to high heaven we could have known him. I often wonder what little Billy would have been like and the sort of man he would have become. What turn would our lives have taken had he lived?

And then there was that young couple from near Woodstock, who'd lost their newborn, wrapped him up, and buried him beneath the soil on top of their grandmother's casket, because, as the father said, "Grandma loved all babies."

Just then a batch of young raccoons raced across the narrow road, hunched like a bunch of kids up to no good. I laughed to beat the band.

"William," announces Hannah, "I feel faint in this heat. I go sit down, yah, yah."

Callie snickers (not in a mean way) and whispers her own version of "Yah, yah," as we watch Hannah totter across the dirt road that circles the cemetery, and wilt onto a bench in the shade of the largest cotton-wood tree in this old section. My God, you'd think she was Greta Garbo the way she presses the back of her hand against her forehead. And her accent is so thick you could ladle it up with a slotted spoon and not lose a bit of it.

Nellie is easier to understand and not so delicate. Not very bright, either, if you ask me. A lot like her father—fixed in opinions, short on imagination. She reminds me of a big old robin, cocking her head as she moves from stone to stone, poking at the crab grass with her cane.

"Where the hell is he, Nellie?" I loosen my tie, and not just because of the heat. "He was supposed to go in next to Grandma and Auntie."

Nellie grumbles something about inappropriate use of "cuss words," stoops over a patch of ground, peers through her bifocals at a pair of small metal plaques, and shouts as if we're all a mile away, "Here they are! Yoo-hoo! Over here, everyone! I found them!"

Hannah gets up too quickly from her bench and staggers toward us, crossing the narrow road like a woman come unhinged. Sad, because I remember when we were kids she used to walk like a country girl trying for a city girl.

I quickly join Nellie and lean over for a closer look at the two tiny plaques barely peeking up at us through thick grass.

"Unacceptable," I mutter, trying to edge the growth away with the toe of my dress shoe. "See here, Cal? Grandma and Auntie aren't even properly marked. These are the same old temporaries that were dropped in right after they died. I remember seeing these as a kid."

Callie's jaw drops. "Is this it?" she asks. "Is this all there is? Not even a last name? Or a birth date?"

I kick once more at the earth around two bronze squares where grass cuticles have taken over. Damned stuff, all matted and thick. I can barely make out the tiny lettering:

MOTHER ERNESTINA 1899	DAUGHTER EDNA 1900

To the left of these, there is only sod. No other marker. Just a patch of grass-covered sod. Like a two-person search party, Callie and I shuffle through the dense blades, hoping to find something more.

"I don't see anything," says Cal, focusing on the ground.

"What the . . . ? There's nothing here for Amer!"

"Sakes alive, William," growls Hannah. "You'll wake the dead."

"I don't care. We had an agreement. If Dad and I brought him back, your folks would set a proper tombstone. What the hell happened?"

"Really, Will, you needn't cuss."

"I can't believe this. No stone for Uncle Amer?"

"Oh, it's all such a puzzle," says Nellie, pursing her thin lips as if sucking on a sourball. This woman, beginning as a youngster, has always looked as though she's been spooned a healthy dose of castor oil.

"You shouldn't blame us," she whines. "We were only young girls when this happened. And don't forget, times were hard back then. You know that, Will. And how's a come you never bothered to return in all these years? Until now, huh?"

"Yah, yah," pipes Hannah, blotting her temples with a starched white hanky edged in pink lace. "I'm afraid we haven't given much thought to this part of the cemetery since our own folks passed. It's all we can do to set flowers for them once a year."

Is she that frail, for heaven's sake? I let my arms droop and focus on Hannah's features to determine if what she says is true and if, in some small way, she's allowing me my own reasons for not having come back to Rockford, until today. I stare at her clear blue eyes and innocent half smile that reveal nothing out of the ordinary. And those dabs of rouge and powder, like white and pink dust caked over soft wrinkles in the heat of the day. Like her mother, she's grown a large, shiny nose and a very stout frame. And yah, yah, she's always had a poker face.

I can't resist saying, "Well, after all, your folks were supposed to see to it that Amer got a suitable burial. That was the deal."

I yank off my necktie and mop my brow with the fresh handkerchief Emily had tucked into my breast pocket earlier this morning, next to a couple of Amer's letters.

"Hell, their folks were too damned Scotch to buy the stones," I whisper to Cal, a little too loudly, perhaps, because she puts a finger to her lips.

"Hush, Dad, they'll hear you."

"Well, some Swedes hold their purse strings pretty damned tight to the vest," I spout, shrugging off my suit jacket and pointing at my right ear. "Shoot! They can't hear me. I don't think there's much juice left in their batteries."

Once again, I poke around on the grass with the toe of my shoe. "How could they just leave it this way? I guess Amer might as well have been lowered into a pauper's grave out West, the way the sheriff said, when no one claims the body. At least there would have been a plain stone marking his site."

Looking a little tired around the eyes, Cal shakes her head. "Oh, Dad. I'm so sorry about all of this. I'm as disappointed as you are."

"It's been seventy years," I say loudly enough for all to hear, "and I'd like some answers. Uncle Frank and Uncle Ed were supposed to plan the funeral service. If my dad paid the undertaker back in Montana, plus our travel expenses bringing Amer home, his brothers said they'd take care of the rest, including a respectable casket and a decent plot. Hell, wouldn't you think that would have included a tombstone? Even a simple one, for Christ's sake—those chea . . ."

"This is the spot. I'm sure of it," says Hannah, wandering back to where Callie and I are standing. "This is where Grandma and Auntie are. As I recall, Amer got put in alongside them, here on the left." She points an arthritic finger at a piece of ground between the curb and those small bronze plaques.

Cal and I scour the plot one more time, on the chance that we've missed some small marker hidden in a portion of crabgrass.

Nellie takes a little pair of shears from her purse, bends over, and tries to clip the coarse, thick grass away from our grandmother's plaque, emitting little grunting sounds with each gouge.

"Oh, for heaven's sake, Nell," says Hannah in a voice tinged with sarcasm. "Those scissors are so dull you could ride to town on them."

Cal laughs into her fist. And I can't help but chuckle.

With great effort, Nellie stands up. Clutching her tiny weapon and waving it high in the air, she tips backwards for a moment, until she can find her equilibrium. Hard to believe these are the same cousins who used to scramble up haymow ladders, swim in oat bins, and gallop their ponies across the fields like Annie Oakley. I, myself, may have slowed down a bit, but not that much.

"So, this is all he got—this little patch of ground," I blurt out. "Not even a temporary, a little bronze plaque like Grandma's and Auntie Edna's. I don't like this one bit. To think that a man who worked acres and acres of land all his life should end up in a plot that seems barely large enough for a child's coffin. And no marker? After what my dad and I went through to bring him home, for Christ's sake!"

I feel light in the head. My heart skips a beat.

"Dad's right," Cal says in a stern voice, moving in close, ready to bolster me if need be. "He and Granddad did their part. There should be something here for Amer."

Taking shallow breaths, I make an effort to hide my sadness as I look from Cal to Nell and Hannah, remembering when Amer first came to live with us on our farm near Hadley, in Southwestern Minnesota—a place we called God's Country.

Chapter 3

Dressed Like a Hussy

GOD'S COUNTRY—THE YEAR, nineteen-aught six, when Uncle Amer came to live with us. My brother and I were little shavers. I was born in aught-three and Ray in aught-two.

Amer had a higher pitched voice than our dad and the occasional mannerisms of Stan Laurel (Laurel & Hardy), including a child-like grin and the vacant twinkle in his eyes beneath arched brows, which made it all the funnier when he told his jokes. From the time we could understand language, he'd have us gather 'round, teach us songs from the operas, read us grown-up books. And tease us. At some level we knew he was kidding, yet we believed everything he said. Even the times he'd ruffle our hair and tell us that Ray, as a newborn, was found in a slough near Bear Lake Woods, hanging around a flock of mallards, until he could figure out which one he wanted to fly in on. I'd ask,

"If my brother came out of a slough on the back of a quacker, where'd I come from, Uncle Amer?" And he'd say,

"You, Willie-boy? Why, you swam all the way through Lake Summit on the tail of a great northern pike."

When I told Uncle Ed (Nellie's father) that my brother and I had come into this world on a duck and a fish, he stared at us, slack-jawed, as if we really had.

Mother and Dad and Uncle Amer made life exciting for Ray and me. For sure, there was hard work to be done on the farm, starting at a young age—six, seven. We had to feed the dogs, gather corncobs for Mother's cook stove, collect eggs from the coop and from the secret places around the farmyard, wherever the chickens decided to lay: inside the machine shed, beneath a tractor, next to a tree in the oak grove. That was like going on a treasure hunt. We went with Dad to check the traps he'd set around Bear Lake Woods, and brought back muskrats, beavers, and an occasional mink. Dad skinned them out, then stretched and nailed their hides to the gray wooden siding of another old shed that doubled as a garage.

Away from the farmyard, next to an open field, Dad and Uncle Amer set up some land for trap shooting. Hunters came from all over Maywood County to practice their leads on clay birds. Hunting dogs, especially Labradors and Chesapeake Bay Retrievers, our own included, sat nearby, eyes focused, muscles aquiver, ready for a command. It didn't take them long to realize it would be a day of rest and play for them while their sharp-eyed shooters competed for trophies and pooled prize money.

"Pull!" called the men in varying pitches. Then came the shotgun blast and clay pigeon fragments raining down from a summer-blue sky topped by white clouds. Sometimes, a black and yellow disc flew far across the field, untouched by shot. A miss like that didn't happen very often.

You could close your eyes and know which man was ready to shoot by the sound of his "Pull!" Uncle Amer had a distinctive call, bordering on the musical. "Pull!" he'd sing out in his tenor voice.

Occasionally, in early evening, my mother Julia would join us, wearing a pair of Dad's pants, baggy on her, and a work shirt. Her long, wavy, black hair she'd pulled back and secured with side combs. Mother was a pretty good shot. It sounded funny, though, to hear her soprano voice call, "Pull!"

Every fall, the men and their dogs came back to hunt pheasants in our cornfields and to fill out on their limits of ducks and geese from nearby sloughs: mallards, teal, redheads, canvasbacks, Canada honkers.

As soon as my brother and I were able to raise a shotgun in a single smooth motion, we stood before our posts and called out in as deep a voice as we could muster, "Pull!" We also took turns at the trap, springing clay pigeons for shooters who rarely missed.

Ray and I competed against each other, kept a running tally from one shoot to the next. Usually, he'd go off someplace to sulk. But with Dad and Uncle Amer, there was no competition; they were equals. Between them, they filled the tack room shelves in our barn with every kind of prize you could win for trap shooting in those days—the early 1900s: framed certificates with curlicue handwriting in black ink faded to brown, hand-stitched blue ribbons, carved balsa wood trophies, bronze medals strung on leather thongs.

When Uncle Amer sauntered across the farmyard with his Ithaca, or stood off to one side of the shooting range, waiting his turn, he always seemed a little vulnerable to me. But as soon as he stood at his post, snapped that twelve-gauge to sight, and leaned into position, he was as staunch and unwavering as the rest of the men.

Now, as I turn away from this little patch of graveyard grass, recalling how Amer had once lived and labored on great stretches of land at home and in Montana, I can't help but shout:

"Listen here! Of all the family, why is it that Amer's the only one who went forgotten?"

Hannah and Nellie shrug and continue gazing at the two existing plaques and at the ground next to them.

I turn to Cal and whisper, "Hell, they can't even look at me. The sins of their fathers—that's what this is all about. A carry-over. Same damned attitude drifted down into the next generation."

"Dad, I feel as badly as you do. I thought for sure we'd find a stone for him—a really nice marker. Maybe we should arrange for one ourselves. What do you think?"

"Thirty-nine years old," I mutter, looking up at the treetops. "Gave it everything he had. If only we'd known sooner. He was such a friendly sort. Shouldn't have had an enemy in the world."

"Well, your folks were awfully protective of him, Will," says Hannah, finally looking in my direction. "He had to try going it alone some time."

"Yes," Nellie sighs, "but he was always a little . . . I don't know . . . peculiar. That's what my mother used to say—awful peculiar. They never really cared for the way . . ."

"What are you talking about?" I feel a surge in blood pressure. "They never cared for what? What's that supposed to mean?" A little woozy, I take hold of Callie's arm

"I only meant . . ."

"For Christ's sake, Nell, he never hurt a living thing! He worked damn hard, hired out to the neighbors when they needed an extra hand. We were lucky to have his help on the farm. Everyone in Leeds Township liked Amer, rooted for him when he played baseball with the Hadley Buttermakers. One of the best pitchers they ever had."

"Well, that may be, but . . ."

"And he was good to us kids. If we dared complain about those long hot days in the fields, we never got a scolding. Oh, we got plenty of that from our folks, but never from Uncle Amer. He always made us laugh. Had a knack for turning hard work into a game, especially during corn picking time. You remember those days, harvesting corn by hand."

"Who could forget?" Hanna snorts. "Suffering under a hot sun. Tough leather wrist huskers lopping off one ear at a time; it was certainly no picnic."

"I remember that story, Dad," says Cal in a bright voice. "You told me about Uncle Amer painting a bull's-eye on the wagon's bang board so you could keep score. Like playing darts with ears of corn."

"Yup, and old Bessie and Fanny pulled the wagon through the corn-rows all by themselves. No driver, no commands. They knew how to set a pace that kept up with ours."

With these threads of memory drifting back into my head, talking about those early years, and casting aside Nellie's comment about Amer, I can even sense the sounds and smells of our farm: the rustle of brittle cornstalks brushing up against our wagon; a skittering pheasant whose wings whistle as he takes to the air; the clunk of dried ears striking the bang board; a pale blue sky with mounded clouds on the distant horizon; field dust coating the sweaty horses whose shaggy hooves flip forward and back, crunching tough roots as the team plods along under a scorching sun.

"Mixed breeds, they were," I tell the ladies. "Bessie and Fanny, part Shire and part Percheron. A fine pair, devoted to our work."

"We had draft horses like that," says Hannah in a sing-song voice, as if trying for a one-up. "Duke and Sadie. Bessie was one of our milk cows, but we always called her in with, 'Here, Boss. Come, Boss.'"

"Everyone had a Bossie in those days," I mutter.

Nellie's eyes narrow as she points her cane at me. "Amer might have made things fun for you and Ray, but don't forget how he acted during that Halloween party we went to one year."

"What do you mean?"

"He had a tendency to take things a little too far, according to Mother and Daddy—showing up at the sale barn dressed like a hussy."

"Of course. All decked out in a mask and wig. So what?"

"A long, blond wig. And balloons tucked under the front of some dress he obviously borrowed from your mother. It was grotesque. That's what my mother said. Why, he was practically . . . I don't know . . . he looked like a . . ."

"It was a masquerade, Nell. Everybody wore a crazy costume. A few of the women dressed like men. Why don't you make something of that?"

"To think he got by with using the women's restroom! Then laughed about it afterward. And the way he walked? My land!"

Nellie stands cockeyed, one hand on her hip like Mae West, who's about to suggest, "Why don't you come up and see me sometime?"

"Nell, your lingo hasn't changed one whit since you were a girl. You sound like an over-the-fence gossip. So what if he played his part? So what?"

"Our folks thought it was disgusting, didn't they, Hannah? Why, I remember Mother and Daddy saying . . ."

"Hell, you remember things you have no business criticizing! He was just having fun, making people laugh. Why, the local paper even featured him."

I don't care for this shift in conversation; makes me feel woozy again. And Cal looks confused. She hasn't heard these details. I've never brought them up. Wouldn't have known quite how to do that anyhow, and so. . . .

"What are you talking about, Dad?" she asks.

"Nothing. Not a damned thing. Amer was just as I've told you, Cal, a fun-loving, hard-working man who shouldn't have had an enemy in the world. And now this." I point at the ground. "Inexcusable!"

Hannah raises a hand like a teacher quieting her class. "I think we should rest for a spell, yah, yah." She shepherds us across the narrow road, toward a pair of sturdy benches.

It takes my cousins forever to sit—such a big production of snapping open their purses, fishing out large handkerchiefs for the occasion and placing them just right on the curved slats of a recently varnished bench. They ease themselves down and fuss with their skirts, arranging the folds until they look like drooping peach and lime green poppies—if there are such things. Nellie sits as straight as a headstone, hands clutching her purse as if she were riding a city bus in a rough neighborhood. Hannah pats the space between, inviting Callie to join them. Good sport that she is, Cal backs up to the bench and laughingly wedges herself between the two elderly women. Hannah chuckles and wraps an arm around Cal's shoulders. Nellie manages one of her castor oil smiles.

To these old eyes, my daughter still looks like a fairly happy girl, even though, not so long ago, she went through some pretty rough patches. She resembles me, I think: shiny hair, almost black (like mine and Emily's used to be), olive skin, eyes the color of a northern lake. You'd never know we're Scandinavian. What is her age now? Forty-two, I believe.

Yes, forty-two last June. Doesn't seem possible. A fine girl, now a woman who, like most everyone, will need to work through her own issues.

At times, Callie still acts like a kid. My fishing buddy. Of course, we haven't been out on a lake since we got caught in that awful rainstorm up north. With all the doctoring I've had to do, my tackle box hasn't seen the light of day in some time. The old Johnson 10-horse hangs from a crosspiece in one corner of the garage at our apartment building, and my Crestliner sits on its trailer behind it, covered with a tarp against the snow and cold, which will come as surely as the geese and ducks return in spring. Sad, though, to see a boat dry-docked, even in winter. She has always done her best by us, speeding, floating, and drifting across Lake Shetek, Pine River, and Norway Lake. And I let everyone know that this honey of a fourteen-foot boat took us through the big waters during that storm on Leech Lake. Frankly, I wasn't sure we'd make it back to shore alive, but I never let Callie know. Seated next to the motor, I just kept smiling at her through the wind and the rain each time she looked up to search my face from her waist-deep bailing spot along the boat bottom.

On our way to Rockford this morning, Cal and I reminisced about that wild adventure on Leech; how she bailed all that incoming water like an automaton, second-guessing my change in direction, wondering if I knew what I was doing at the throttle. We can laugh about it now, yet we'll never forget how that fierce wall of water charged at us from across the bay with a mean sky behind it. Sudden whitecaps turned into monstrous rollers that broke over the stern of our small fishing boat. I'm so glad that Cal didn't let that experience deter her from going out on the water again. But then, I knew she wouldn't.

In fact, she told me about a silly thing she'd done last November:

"I wanted to go swimming," she said.

"What? In November?"

"Well, yah. The sun was out and the air felt really warm that day while I was sitting on the hillside with Piper, overlooking the bay. So I changed into shorts and a tee-shirt, went down to the water's edge and eased myself onto my favorite boulder, ready to jump in. But I could only manage to enter as far as my knees. My feet and ankles and calf muscles locked up, began to freeze, so I had to get out."

"Well, I would guess so, Cal, at least for several months."

"Come April or May, I think I'll be able to make it," she said. "At least up to my hips. Or maybe even my waist."

It seemed as though Callie was talking about a different kind of survival, and that it would take some time to recover from what she'd been through. Anyhow, that's how I see it.

Today, she seems to enjoy being the pampered girl, acquiring a greater sense of the half of her that's Swedish. We got a good dose of the Old Country upon our arrival here in Illinois. Hannah and Nellie welcomed us with bosomy hugs and a wonderful lunch of homemade meatballs, limpa bread, and rice pudding with lingonberry sauce; hard to beat a meal like that. Cal's eyes sparkled as the four of us sat down together amid old treasured plates and a bright silver service. And my cousins' lilting accents. I felt like a boy again, minding my manners at the same lace-covered cherry wood table set with the same fragile china and that herd of red, blue, and yellow Dala horses standing stiff-leggèd in the center. Some things never change from one generation to the next. Some good, some not so good.

Now, sitting on the bench in the cemetery, beneath the cottonwood branches, Hannah smiles and playfully butts shoulders with Cal.

"Yah, yah. I'm so glad you came along with your papa. We like getting to know you."

Yes, Hannah is a lot like her father, Frank—able to find humor in her days, managing to extend a little warmth. But then there's Nellie—old sobersides, rigid as a fence post, her mouth like a Vise-Grip. Must run in that side of the family. Uncle Ed, her father, seldom cracked a smile. And neither did her mother.

"What will you choose when the time comes?" Nellie asks of no one in particular. "Burial or cremation?"

Callie frowns slightly at a subject she shouldn't as yet have to consider.

"A hell of a thing to bring up, Nell." I scowl at my cousin. "I don't know. Haven't thought about it." (Actually, I have, but I don't care to discuss it).

Raising an eyebrow, Hannah tisk-tisks and says, "Well, old girl, do you think everyone's going to rise again? Stand around these monuments and clap their hands?"

Nellie purses her thin lips and twiddles her thumbs. "My, oh my. Guess we won't know 'til we get there."

I snort at their lingo and lean over to contemplate the lavender and yellow wildflowers threading themselves through the wrought iron base of my bench. As much as I've appreciated my cousins' initial hospitality upon our arrival, I've never been able to abide a babbling old biddy.

After casting off my irritation, I look up to see what the wind is doing. Callie, trying to suppress a complicit smile, glances overhead, alert to the strong breeze pushing through big pines. The wind stirs up the cottonwood leaves, making them tremble like a thousand fluttering hands—an audience applauding a stellar performance. I prefer to imagine that the applause is for Uncle Amer and the fact that nothing could have prevented him from boarding that west-bound train to Montana.

Lingering here in this cemetery brings to mind not only Uncle Amer, but other family members long dead—especially the man whose behavior, and wife and daughter's untimely deaths, greatly affected their five sons, including my father and Amer.

"What do you know about August?" I ask my cousins. "The old Swede who was our grandfather? All my life, I've wondered why he lit out, abandoning his family of six, including our dads, Uncle Amer, Uncle Reno, and daughter Edna."

"I never heard much talk about him," says Hannah, "except that one day he just up and left."

"Daddy refused to discuss it," says Nellie, "so we gave up asking. Awful, just awful for a man to leave his family like that, and having so many sons who needed him. Especially Reno, their youngest."

Of course, all that happened around 1898, several years before my cousins and my brother and I were born. But Grandfather August was the talk of our family all the while I was growing up. Grandma thought he'd returned to Sweden, until one of the boys spotted him two counties over, with another 'wife' and a second herd of children.

Learning about her husband's secret life was more than Grandma Ernestine could endure. She never smiled again, and died within a year. That left young Edna in charge of her five brothers. She caught the influenza and died shortly after her seventeenth birthday. Those bronze markers across the way belong to them: Ernestine and Edna.

After that, the boys parted company. As my dad and Uncle Amer used to explain, "We all drifted away like sagebrush before the wind."

Frank and Ed wandered around the Dakotas for a few years before settling in Illinois. Uncle Reno, as rumor had it, set himself up as a ladies' man in San Francisco, shot craps, and frequented opium dens in Chinatown. And then there was Amer, who farmed with my dad before striking out on his own. All different kinds of sagebrush.

"What really happened to Uncle Amer?" asks Hannah. "We were never as close to him as you and your brother were. Over the years, we only heard bits and pieces."

"My folks," chimes Nellie, "blamed it on that part of the country—too wild, they said. Mother said he never should have gone to Montana. 'A place like that?' she said. 'Why, it wasn't safe. He should have stayed at home where everybody knew him.'"

"Well, he's home now, Nellie," says Hannah, pulling a face as she motions toward his supposèd gravesite across the road.

"Sempty years," I murmur, pronouncing the number the way my mother used to say it. "Tucked under that corner piece of sod. And not one mark to let the world know who he was."

"Tell us, Will," says Nellie. "We'd like to hear more about him, wouldn't we, Hannah?"

"Yah, yah. But wouldn't it be more comfortable if we went back to the house?" Hannah shifts her ample behind on the bench in an exaggerated way. "I could put on the coffee and then..."

"Nope, we're gonna stay right where we are." I nod at the gravesites and reach into my suit coat pockets for bundles of yellowed envelopes—letters from Amer—and for my pipe and tobacco. "Right where we are," I repeat, tamping a bowlful. "It's the least we can do for him. No, siree, I won't be telling Amer's story over lace doilies and teacups."

Touching a lighted match to the tobacco, I draw on my briar and wink at Cal who watches the smoke trail off on the wind, just as she did during her childhood. My Callie girl—in on all these stories since she was a little tyke.

My cousins look miffed, but I don't care. Let 'em grumble. They sigh and fuss with their skirts, then settle back, finally ready to listen. They'll be all right. These benches are comfortable here in the shade. And I have plenty of sweet tobacco.

Chapter 4

A Terrific Fever

I WAS ONLY SIXTEEN at the time, yet I can recount every detail from the minute we got the telegram until the day we brought Amer to Rockford for burial. But first, I want you to know about our uncle when he was alive.

Picture him loping across the yard toward our house—a square, two-story stucco farmhouse—waving his arms, clutching a fistful of brochures. That afternoon he'd ridden Bessie into Hadley, to the Enge-bretson Brother's store and post office, and couldn't wait to show us what had arrived all the way from Saint Paul.

Amer had caught a terrific fever. Not the sick kind like scarlet fever, but the type that makes a fellow antsy, lights up his eyes with possibili-ties—the kind of fever that sends a man westward.

At age thirty-eight, four years younger than my dad, he still looked like a boy, slender with thin wrists hanging from the frayed cuffs of a blue chambray shirt bleached pale from dozens of hot water washings. His eyes were the same color as that shirt. He had light brown hair that always looked trimmed as if a big popcorn bowl had been plopped on top of his head and someone scissored off whatever stuck out below, then shaved the stubble. Amer's face was tanned, except for his forehead, as pale as winter wheat. We all looked like that during those prickly hot summer days working in the fields.

Too old to go to war, my uncle seemed content to stay on with us, farming our rich southern Minnesota soil—good black loam. Until the fall of 1918, it seemed as though Amer would always be a part of our immediate family. But then that Montana fever took over and nothing could bring it down. It all started with the set of broadsides he'd sent away for, dated September of that year. Within a few months, our uncle would be leaving us, taking the first leg of his journey to the depot in Pipestone for that fateful "All aboard!"

The day those brochures arrived was like a smorgasbord. In place of fancy food, a feast of possibilities. Mother had just finished washing up the dinner dishes and had gone upstairs to work on her mending. Dad was checking on the corn in a field close to the fence behind our house. Ray and I were tossing an old kittenball, playing keep-away with Sport and Docky, our Border Collie and Chesapeake hunting dog, when Amer clip-clopped up the lane, urging Bessie along as fast as a workhorse can trot. He slid off her, scattering a klatch of squawking chickens on his way to the house, keeping pace with the dogs who joined the race. Ray and I were right behind as Amer called over his shoulder, "C'mon, boys, got something to show ya!" He took the steps three at a time and burst into the kitchen, shouting, "Vic! Julia!"

Out of breath, he cleared the long table, moved the big sugar bowl, saltcellar, and jar of spoons over to the cupboard, then scrubbed the oilcloth, rubbing it down as if to erase its blue checkered pattern. With a flourish, he spread his set of colored brochures from one end to the other, and with the sweep of an arm showed us what he was so excited about. What he'd been dreaming of for weeks: a land rush program in Eastern Montana, sponsored by the Chicago, Milwaukee and Saint Paul railroads, in connection with the Illinois Central and Great Northern transcontinental passenger trains. An invitation to heaven.

A farmer's paradise, proclaimed one folder, *A land and wheat bonanza*. Imagine getting in on that! As fast as the gandy dancers could pummel in those spikes, new lines snaked across open territory, all the way to Seattle.

"Who's James J. Hill?" I asked, noticing the name printed on each of the broadsides.

Amer held one up toward the ceiling. "A famous railroad tycoon," he said. "Offering free passage to lucky honyockers."

"What's a honyocker?" asked Ray.

"The opposite of a James J. Hill," answered our dad, just in from the cornfield. "A poor sodbuster hoping to strike it rich."

We came to find out that the term was a mean one. Derogatory. But Amer enjoyed saying it, always emphasizing the first syllable—HON-yocker—until the word floated around like any other and lost its negative meaning.

As if he were already on his way to broader horizons, Amer stepped in front of the kitchen window. Reading aloud from one of the pamphlets, he reached up as if to string his words through the windowpanes and across the treetops out there in the distant grove:

"'Come see the beautiful Yellowstone River, the booming town of Forsyth, and Custer County. Only three days by train and stage.'

"Now what sort of fellow could resist that?" he asked, leaning against the cook stove, arms crossed. "You've got this farm under control, Vic. And the boys have been working the fields and tending livestock like grown men for some time. I've just got to go out there and try my luck. If I don't catch hold of it now, I might never go. Might never make it."

Our dad was quiet for a moment. "Well," he said in his drawn-out way, "we won't hold you back."

Uncle Amer's Adam's apple bobbed up and down a few times before his wide grin overrode a brief look of apology.

"Thank you, Vic."

He turned to look at our mother who had been standing next to the table, holding a yellow and white checked apron that she had been sewing. At first, she looked a bit startled.

"And Julia," said Amer, "I hope you'll be happy for me."

She smiled, set the apron and thread on the table, and gave our uncle a hug. "Gather up any of your clothes that need mending," she said.

From then on, Uncle Amer acted like us boys—Ray was sixteen and I was fifteen—fidgety, full of energy, running with Sport and Docky around the farmyard, dancing about the parlor to mother's piano playing in the evenings; I can still picture him waving his arms, waltzing in circles, back and forth, then onto the porch with Strauss and his "Tales from the Vienna Woods."

A gifted pianist, ever since she was a young girl, my mother had hoped to go study in Vienna. But there was no money, and so she spent the rest of her life as a home parlor performer, sharing her dream.

Amer could hardly sleep at night. He mostly sat up figuring out how much it would cost for seed, workhorses, field equipment, and the drilling of a well. In Eastern Montana, lumber was at a premium—there were no bountiful woods. He'd have to build a sod house.

"A sod house?" I asked. "What's that?"

"Just what it sounds like."

"No, but wouldn't it cave in on you if it rains and snows?"

"Not if you build it properly. I'll have to study up on how to do it."

In the early hours of a morning, if Ray or I had forgotten our chamber pot downstairs and had to go to the outhouse, we'd see a light beneath Amer's door. And hear the folding and unfolding of those brochures and the eager scratching of pencil against paper.

So, naturally, my brother and I caught the fever too. We had never known anyone who'd traveled such a far distance on a train before. Well, there was Mrs. Gus Block, who lived on a farm three miles northwest of us. But she only rode the rails as far as Granite Falls in order to help take care of her dying grandmother.

Once, Ray and I each set a penny on the tracks to see what would happen when the train wheels ran over them. We kept the flattened coins in tiny boxes inside our dresser drawer. We only did that once, because Mother and Dad reminded us that the family couldn't afford to throw money away like that.

Sometimes my brother and I edged along the rails as if we were walking a tightrope—heel-to-toe, heel-to-toe—faster and faster, skating up from behind to push the other off, trying to balance until one or both of us tipped and lost our footing, took flight for a second, then tumbled and glanced off the stones next to the track. Laughing and shouting, we ended up with a roll through thick grass and weeds, down the slope, and into a soggy ditch.

It seemed like a sort of graduation after we studied each broadside for ourselves, imagining what it would be like riding inside one of those beautiful trains; a long stretch of cars curving around mountainsides, running alongside full and rushing rivers, pulled by powerful engines with cowcatchers on the front. Great black engines bound for glory.

I took up my new C-melody saxophone and tried to imitate the sound of those steel wheels rolling along the tracks and that long, drawn-out whistle:

Chooga-chugga, chooga-chugga, whoooa-whoooo

What must the real thing sound like echoing through those canyons?

The next morning at breakfast, Amer seemed more confident than ever while laying out his plan in detail. He would stake a 360-acre claim in Eastern Montana, north of Forsyth, somewhere between the little towns of Edwards and Jordan, and work the land until he could prove up on it.

"I'll be able to declare homestead within three years' time," he told us. Actually, he repeated his detailed plans many times over: during breakfast, dinner, lunch, and supper. I suppose he thought the more often he talked about them, the quicker those three years would peel away from his calendar and he'd own the land.

"Why, who knows? I might even build me a fine ranch by then." He tapped the side of his head with a long, sharp pencil. "I already have the drawings pictured up here."

At that moment, Ray and I desperately wanted to go along. Seated across the table from Amer, we jiggled around in our chairs until you'd think we suffered from the Saint Vitus Dance. We were ready to pack our own bags. Although knowing how much we were needed at home, we argued and pleaded with Dad to let us go along.

Amer laughed at our boyish outbursts and goaded us on, until Mother brought Ray and me up short with a scolding and painful tugs on our ears.

All Dad ever had to do to get his boys in line was fix us with a pale blue-eyed stare and murmur, "Ip-ip-ip." He made it clear that we had to finish school. "Amer will write," he said, "and let us know all about the land."

"Then maybe some day," said Mother, "you can travel out there to see him. I wonder, though, about that part of the country."

"If the soil is as rich as James J. Hill says it is," said Amer, "even half as good as what we've got here, well . . . once I get my patent, you can all come for a visit. Who knows, you might even decide to stay on. I have a hunch there's going to be no place quite like Montana."

At some level, Amer must have known about the poor soil and drought conditions, the severe winters when prairie chickens and livestock froze to death, the demands of building a sod hut and managing livestock. But he was hooked on the idea of his own place; its possibilities; the beauty of it all. You see, he was a Romantic who quoted from Emerson to prove his point: "'Life invests itself with inevitable conditions, which the unwise seek to dodge . . . All the good of nature is the soul's, and may be had if paid for in nature's lawful coin, that is, by labor which the heart and the head allow.'"

Although my uncle often talked about the facets of compensation from Emerson's essay, there was one line he never acknowledged, at least to us: "If the good is there, so is the evil."

Mother and Dad were happy for Amer, but not full out. I could tell they were worried. He was a strong, hard worker. But there was something different about him; something not typical of the countryside folks. Whatever the chores—milking cows, manning a harrow, plowing up a garden for Mother's flowers and vegetables—he moved differently:

fluid-like, with a certain grace like those swans on Pine River, where Cal and I fished for several summers.

He wasn't like the other farmers in the area, around Masterton, Hadley, and Lake Wilson—especially those big Norwegians who seemed a little clumsy as they went about their lighter tasks. At the end of the day, once they'd finished the demanding, rhythmic picking of corn by hand, shocking hay, grubbing tree stumps, trudging along behind a plow and their team of workhorses through cloddy fields, those same farmers, toward dusk, moved like cripples across their yards. With buckets of oats and well water for the livestock gripped in gnarled hands, their gaits were pronounced by pained hitches, as if they had to will their backs and legs not to give out. Whereas Amer, light on his feet, seemed to dance through his evening chores.

The week before our uncle left, in March of 1919, Ray and I paid special attention to all of our 'last times' together: the last time we ice-fished on Lake Summit where bands of Sioux Indians used to camp, and where we found arrowheads in the spring; the last climb into our haymow to pitch feed down for the livestock; the last milk stream contest between Sport and Docky.

While we milked the cows, Amer had trained Sport and Docky, our Border Collie and Chessie, to stand opposite the dung trough, back of the stanchions. As soon as he shouted, "Ready, Set, Go!," the dogs—wild-eyed, jaws snapping, jowls flapping—lapped up the long, steamy squirts of milk we shot their way.

Some evenings, after chores, we put on musicales. Mother had saved up her egg money to send away for the latest sheet music from Minneapolis and Chicago: "Beautiful Dreamer," "Seated One Day at the Organ," "Mister Dunderback." She also ordered songs from the great operas: Puccini's arias "Un Bel Dì" from *Madama Butterfly*, "O Mio Babbino Caro," from *Gianni Schicchi*, and "Nessun Dorma" from *Turandot*. Although she didn't have a great voice, Mother especially liked to sing "O Mio Babbino Caro." And so did the rest of us.

Oh, how we loved Puccini. Amer once said he wished he looked like him. Mother thought he was just about the handsomest man she'd ever seen, besides my father, of course. Giacomo Puccini's picture was printed on the front of her sheet music; he had sensual and knowing eyes, thick dark hair, a nicely trimmed mustache, and full lips. Mother and Amer, who played violin, sang Puccini so often, the rest of us couldn't help but repeat those Italian words—*O mio babbino caro, mi piace è bello, bello*—even though we had no idea what they meant.

Although none of us, except Amer, had quite the heart for it, we put on a regular gala the night before he left. Mother warbled and played accompaniment on our Chicago upright, a big old box of a piano. Dad kept time and danced around the parlor. Ray buzzed the tunes on a fine-tooth comb wrapped in tissue paper (sounding a bit like our mother's voice). I played my C-melody, a saxophone I'd saved up for in order to form a small band with a few of my high school buddies.

If walls were ever capable of storing such things, those making up our sturdy farmhouse would remember that music as long as they stood— especially Mother's flamboyant piano technique, Amer's tenor voice, and the plaintive notes from his violin.

About our favorite tune, "O Mio Babbino Caro," out in 1918, Amer said, "Now there's a song that would like to make you cry." He couldn't get the piece out of his head. And neither could we. He'd sing it while shaving or skipping down the steps for breakfast or balancing on a milking stool, one side of his face tight against a cow's warm flank, certain that the herd would give more milk if he gave them his music.

Amer sang loudest in the middle of a field, sounding like Enrico Caruso as he trudged along behind Fanny and Bessie: "O mio babbino caro, mi piace è bello, bello." With rounded vowels and a haunting melody in ¾ time, that aria took hold deep inside us. We were careful, Ray and I, that no one should see how our eyes watered whenever we heard our uncle sing that song.

Oh, they sang for their supper that last night—Amer and his fiddle and Puccini.

Chapter 5

All Aboard!

THAT FINAL MORNING came too soon for Ray and me. Excited and sorry at the same time, we hung around to watch Amer finish packing. He didn't have much: his Victrola and records, books, some clothing (that Mother had mended), and his beloved violin, a Farny with ivory inlay, wrapped in a clean feedsack.

In those days, Dad had an Overland Automobile, a 1914 model 79 Roadster. But it held only two people plus some stowage, so Ray and I hitched up the horses and loaded Amer's belongings onto the wagon, then hopped up and settled in next to the luggage, grinning and poking at each other in our excitement. Mother and Dad sat on the bench next to Amer, who drove the team. Sitting up straight and holding the reins lightly, he guided Bessie and Fanny along the gravel road from our farm to the Hadley depot. My parents were quiet during the short ride. Because Ray and I were propped up behind them, leaning against a bag and a suitcase, we could only imagine the expressions on each of their faces. I felt the adventure rippling across the fields and pretended that I would be hopping onto the train alongside my uncle.

We arrived at the depot just in time for Amer to purchase his ticket before we heard that awful and wonderful announcement: "All aboard!"

Amer was the only passenger leaving from Hadley station that day, on to Pipestone, then Granite Falls via The Great Northern. From there, Montana!

Never one to show his feelings, Dad simply shook hands with his brother and wished him well. Ray and I helped Amer with his luggage. He hugged Mother, shook hands with my brother and me, gave us each a little hug, then climbed aboard and, after stowing his things, walked down the aisle of the first car to an empty seat. From a lowered window, he flashed a smile that framed his straight, white teeth.

Dad stood next to the tracks, looking a bit downcast. Mother blew kisses, whipped her white handkerchief through the air, and sang out, "Promise to write!"

As the train inched away from the depot, Amer waved broadly from the open window. "You'll hear from me!"

To the rhythm of the engine, Ray and I danced and chanted, "Amer's leaving, Amer's leaving . . ." We jumped and waved and hollered until our socks sagged to our ankles and our voices fractured. Then, as the caboose made its turn past the willow trees and rolled out of sight, our voices trailed off: "Amer's leav-ing, Amer's leav-ing, Amer's leav-ing."

And then he was gone.

All four of us were quiet as we returned to the horses and made our way back to the farm, hearing only those four wagon wheels crunching against gravel, an occasional snort from Bessie or Fanny, a swish of a tail, and the rhythmic sounds of hooves along the trail.

Eventually, this first, long-awaited envelope arrived, postmarked Jordan, Montana, The Treasure State. It was like magic getting mail from the seat of Garfield County—a land of deep river canyons and prairie wilderness. That day, and from then on, whenever we received a letter from Amer, the four of us dropped whatever we were doing and gathered around the kitchen table while Mother read it aloud:

From Fergus Falls to Valley City, North Dakota, the land begins to roll. The great Missouri River marked my passage and welcomed me into western country—Mandan and Custer land. The small buttes of western North Dakota grow massive near Miles City, Montana. And now here I am in Jordan country, "The Big Open."

I imagined Amer taking in those sights through the train window, and tried to picture such exotic territory, those changing land formations that really begin in North Dakota. I could just see Amer bursting with anticipation as he went over his list of needs for building a new life: equipment and horses to purchase, land to work up for a first planting, a shelter to build, water to locate.

How many of those so-called "honyockers" felt uneasy and had second thoughts about leaving the familiar in order to tackle the unknown, carrying only a few simple possessions and their life's savings? If Amer ever felt that way, he never let on. Jokes and music and a flurry of activity covered up any misgivings he might have had. His letters did the same. It was only later that we could read between the lines.

But those early letters contained the same optimism and sense of accomplishment Amer used to show when we laid the corn by every summer—after that last round with the cultivator when the shoots have grown into thriving stalks tall enough to go it on their own. Corn borers and birds and other predators lived off some of the crop. We had to allow for that. But after our final round, it was simply a matter of waiting for the rest of it to grow up. And then came harvest time.

NELLIE EDGES FORWARD from her spot on the bench. "I remember when Daddy laid our corn by," she says. "Once it was planted and cultivated, he could finally find the time to drive us into Rockford so we could see a show."

Slightly startled by Nellie's interjection, I nod in agreement and take a moment to relight my pipe.

"For us," I tell the ladies, "planting time was a regular celebration. Amer would spread his arms as if introducing those young stalks to the world. 'They're taking off on their own now, boys,' he'd say, 'so just sit back and watch 'em grow.'

"Ray and I would run to the pump house, plunge our arms up to the shoulders in that icy water and pull out bottles of Grape Nehi and Orange Crush and beers for Dad and Uncle Amer. Then we'd flop down on our bellies at the edge of the field and spy on the corn, certain we could detect a wobble in those yellow-green blades inching upward from the soil like tiny charmed snakes."

"And did they grow?" asks Cal with a little smirk. "Before your very eyes?"

"Certainly. If you had the patience to lie there long enough on a windless day and set your sights on a tiny mark, why, yes, you could see it happen. Even when a shoot first broke through the soil, we could catch it dancing a slow waltz. Just a little bitty thread bending and rising toward the sunshine."

"Aw, Dad, is that true?"

"Could be. You have to devote a chunk of time, though, to check it out."

"Yah, yah," says Hannah, "I've seen such a thing myself. Long ago."

"Bah, I can just picture you," says Nellie, rolling her eyes. "There lies Hannah in the middle of a field, watching the corn grown."

"Yah, of course. Why not?"

"What would the neighbors say? Whatever would the townsfolk think?"

Hannah giggles. "They'd probably assume that I'd kicked the bucket."

"Yah, yah, toes turned up to the daisies."

"All right, Nell," says Hannah. "Let's get back to . . ."

"Or out there with some guy," Nellie persists. "Or gone around the bend, on your way to the funny farm."

"Yah, yah, that'll do, that'll do. Now let Willie get back to his story."

AMER'S LETTERS read like chapters from a fascinating book. We could hardly wait for the next one to arrive.

Here's a line he wrote about Miles City. Don't you love the sound of that name? Miles City.

A bustling town in a valley surrounded by buttes colored with sunshine, shadows and a thousand shades of rose and ochre above sagebrush and laurel.

This letter especially tells what it was like for Uncle Amer early on:

I arrived in Forsyth, population 7,624, and stopped by the land office to sign the necessary papers and pay my filing fee of ten dollars. The acreage that I'll prove up on in exchange for my labor is near a couple of little burgs called Edwards and Jordan, north of Forsyth. The buttes are gone now, with only low mountains in the distance.

It took plenty of time and money to line up supplies. Some of the folks here are very critical of us "sodbusters." Many are helpful, but a few have had their fill of settlers flooding the land. And they let it be known. Too many families come unprepared for what lay ahead. A few act as if they're on vacation. Others grow desperate. But I think most are aware of what they need to do in order to make it with the land. And survive!

I'm now the proud owner of a buckboard, four draft horses, some field equipment, and tools for building my sod house and digging a well. I might have to hire a driller. Some fellas told me they had to go down as far as two or three hundred feet to find water. I wonder if that's the case, or even possible where my homestead will be.

I purchased a local history book at the General Store, so as to study up on this land I'll be calling "home." Had to laugh when the proprietor proffered his opinion about the great Missouri: "That river," he said, "runs through two-thirds the length of our state. Too thick to drink, too thin to cultivate."

Well then, I told him, I'll just have to cultivate the land and figure out how to find water for me and my animals.

Two of the horses are Belgian, said to be strong and tough. The other two are smaller and younger, part saddle horse, part Percheron. I can ride them, but they're also fit to work the fields.

I've got a good rifle and a Smith and Wesson .45, six shot plus cartridges. I'm not comfortable with a revolver, but one of the sodbusters I met up with said I should carry a sidearm. He said you never know what a man might come up against out here. Well, we'll see about that.

Imagine what I looked like sitting up high on a loaded wagon, giddyuppin' my team across the Forsyth-Yellowstone river bridge and onto the long open trail, north as the crow flies. An endless brown ribbon cutting across the land. There's nothing like it back home.

Whenever I spot a stretch of long grass or wheat rolling with the wind, it reminds me of our big sloughs near Hadley, and the waves on Lake Summit. I've never been on an ocean, but living out here in Eastern Montana might be the closest thing to one—a dry-land sea with plenty of elbowroom.

Toward evening of the first day out, the sky turned deep violet, a backdrop for the livestock grazing in the distance: cattle, of course, and sheep with the longest wool I've ever seen. The cattle were so still along the hillcrest and lower buttes, they seemed like cardboard cutouts against that sky.

I saw some hawks, one bobcat and a lot of mule deer around the dried up creek beds, especially at dusk, but they skittered as soon as I drew near.

Those deer have large mule-like ears and are brownish-gray in color with white rump patches and small black-tipped white tails. I even saw some shedded antlers lying on the ground. With those several tines, they looked like strange branches.

What unsettled me was the sight of so many animal carcasses along the trail and deeper into the land. That tells you how rugged it is out here. I've never seen such vast country nor felt so alone, although I'm sure I'll get used to it.

You should see the sky at night! It's huge and filled with the brightest stars I've ever seen. By comparison, Minnesota seems closed in, as if a canopy were drawn over it. In this part of Montana, the sky is broader than you can imagine, and never-ending, just like the land. A three-quarter moon is practically enough to read by. But when the sky is like pitch and there is no moon, the stars will do the job. . . .

It took Amer two days to cover the distance from Forsyth to Jordan, stopping off-trail where he could water and graze his horses, and camp for the night. Several weeks went by before we heard from him again. That's when he told us about his neighbors:

I have good neighbors. The McKammans are well established and live in a soddy across the road and down a quarter of a mile. They appear to be in their forties or fifties. I like to hear their Irish brogue. John is helping me get started, calls me "Swede." Mary frets about how thin I am. She bakes the most delicious pies from apples or berries that she gathers here and there.

She certainly sees that I eat my share.

A young shepherd dog found his way to my place. I don't know where he came from, didn't seem to have a home to go back to. I named him Radge. He's a fine one, makes for good company. I call the horses Rounder and Sam, Johnny and Skeeky. Does that ring a bell, Julia? Johnny and Skeeky? They aren't like Bessie and Fanny, but they'll come around in due time. I'm pretty tired by nightfall, so after a long day's work, I flop down on the ground with Radge by my side, watch the stars, and figure out tomorrow's list.

I plan to buy a few head of cattle in a year or so . . .

"GOODNESS SAKES ALIVE!" says Hannah, standing up from the bench to stretch her arms and legs. "His letters make that corner of the world sound like heaven."

Nellie sniffs. "If it weren't for all those dead animals along the way."

"I'll bet the hunting was terrific," says Cal. "Wonder if there are any good fishing lakes around there."

"Some, but nothing like what we have in Minnesota. Amer did write about Fort Peck, a big lake connected to the Missouri River, about twenty-six miles north of Jordan. He wanted to go there, try for some walleye and lake trout, but it was way too far."

"Twenty-six miles?" says Nellie. "That's not so far."

"It was back in those days. Besides, he couldn't spare the time." I pick out another envelope from the small stack next to me on the bench. "There are plenty of rivers out there, a little closer to where he lived, like Big Dry Creek, perfect for fly-fishing. I've only cast my line in lakes, though. Well, except for Pine River, that is."

"Where's that?" asks Hannah.

"Central Minnesota. Emily and I used to spend a lot of time up there. But you know, I'd sure like to try a few of those western rivers sometime. That would be like heaven—out there in the wild."

Me too," says Cal, leveling an imaginary cast. She laughs when I ask her if she got a backlash.

"Our family news sent to Uncle Amer generally came from Mother's hand. Here's one of the notes she sent to him:"

Vic and the boys have been out hunting. They brought back three prairie chickens and I roasted them for supper last night. After chores on Saturday, Willie and Ray hiked to Lake Summit and caught a mess of bullheads. They wished you were here with us. Me too. We miss you at the table and talk about how you always like your fish fried up nice and crispy. Can't you just smell them cooking?

With Mary McKamman helping out, we no longer need to imagine you as desperate as a mouse in winter, chewing on a dishtowel that dried a greasy pan or covered a rising loaf!

We've had some very good weather; the corn and beans are coming along fine. Vic and the boys managed to seed some oats and put in a piece of flax. The neighbor's oats across the road are up—one of the first fields around. Willie got the garden tilled for planting the seeds we saved from last year's vegetables.

We wonder how you are doing out there by yourself. Such hard work for one. And so far away. It isn't easy being separated from family. Wish I could have returned to Rockford just once before my mother and father passed on. Long distances are powerful hard. . . .

"Powerful hard," I repeat, looking up at my cousins and feeling a little sadness creep in. "Long distances."

"What makes you say that?" asks Nellie.

"My mother, Julia. She was just a young woman when she had to leave her family behind here in Illinois."

"How come?"

"It was Dad who decided to move to Minnesota, for the hunting and fishing. That was shortly after my brother and I were born. Obviously, we were grateful for the move, but I'll never forget how hard it was on Mother."

I explained that for the first few years, while our farmhouse was being built, we lived in a timbered garage on that acreage north of Hadley. Mother never got over being uprooted, separated from her parents and brothers and sisters. She cried a lot when Ray and I were little boys. Even when we grew older, we would sometimes catch her crying.

With everyone quiet for a moment here in the cemetery, I feel a sudden pang of loneliness for my mother, even though she's been gone for nearly thirty years, buried in the cemetery north of Masterton, alongside my dad. That feeling never goes away, no matter how long it's been—just as it is with Uncle Amer.

"It feels strange," I tell the ladies, "that I've already grown past my parents' ages when they died. Makes no difference how old I am, though. Still seems like yesterday."

"That's for sure," says Nellie, nodding and pointing in the direction of her family plot.

"How long has Vic been gone?" asks Hannah. "We drove up to Minnesota for his funeral, but it's been so long, I've forgotten the particulars."

Thirty-four years. The tenth of May, 1952."

"I was only eight years old," says Cal. "Still, I remember how hard it was to realize I'd never see Granddad again."

Nellie shuffled her feet back and forth beneath the bench. "What took him?" she asks.

I nod at Callie, recalling how troubling it was for her—for all of us.

"Wrong type blood transfusion," I say, feeling that familiar touch of desperation. "But we could never prove it. He came through his operation just fine. Prostate surgery. Didn't take him long to find his old self when we visited him in the recovery room. Mother walked over to his bedside saying, 'Vic, this is Julia. Do you recognize me, Vic? It's Julia, your wife.' At first, Dad pretended to be groggy. 'Julia?' he whispered. 'Julia?' Then he turned his head to squint at Mother, at the gold trim edges along her two front teeth.

"It was the slight grin that gave him away. 'Julia?' he said, 'I'd know your hide if it was tacked to the garage.' "

Nellie frowns. Hannah laughs politely. Only Cal fully understands the affection behind those words.

"They lived at Lake Shetek back then," she says. "Tepeeotah. A great place for Gram and Gramp, because they loved to fish together."

"That's right. Most evenings, you'd find Mother and Dad at the end of their dock, sitting side by each. But that wasn't going to happen again. You see, immediately after his blood transfusion, Dad took a turn for the worse. He was the last of the brothers to go."

"Amer was the first," says Hannah.

"And our dads in between," adds Nellie. "No one knows what became of Uncle Reno."

"Probably faded away inside that opium den in Chinatown," says Cal. "I've always been intrigued by what his life must have been like out there in San Francisco: craps, opium, brothels."

"My, oh my," says Nellie with a frown. "The complete opposite of Uncle Amer."

Cal nods her head. "I would say so."

Unfortunately, as a grade-schooler, Callie overheard some discussions among family members, including her mother and me. She used to hide in a corner beneath the dining room table in order to take it all in, unobserved. Way too often, I think. She also managed to discover a few letters passed along from relative to relative that detailed what had been going on with Uncle Reno in San Francisco's Chinatown. She had even gotten into trouble when her teacher discovered a sheet of paper on top of her classroom desk, containing those unique, foreign-like words that must have intrigued Cal, causing her to create a short list, including "August, abandon, opium, craps, and brothel." I don't think she knew what they all meant. That is, until she reached for a dictionary.

I don't like to reveal such thoughts and say such words, especially in front of the ladies, but Reno (whom I'd never met), rarely in touch with my family, was hanging around out there in Chinatown, focusing on houses of prostitution (both whites and Chinese), gambling, doing opium, and checking out, not only brothels, but "Joss Houses," places of pagan worship.

"We were all just sick about what had happened to him," I tell the women, who were staring at me with wide eyes, especially Hannah and Nellie. "He was such a good looking man with great potential—or so we were told long ago by Frank and Ed. My dad and Uncle Amer didn't seem to know as much about their kid brother as your dads did."

"Well, there were letters from San Francisco, but we were never allowed to read them or hear them read aloud," says Nellie. "Mother kept 'em in a locked drawer, explaining that the writing was all a jumble like some foreign language I wouldn't be able to understand."

"The fact that Grandfather August had abandoned the family," says Hannah, "and then their mother and sister died, seemed to have left Reno the worst off. Anyhow, that's my guess."

"Yah, yah," says Nellie. "I can see that. Especially since he was the youngest of the five boys remaining."

As I relit my pipe filled with rich cherry tobacco, the thought crossed my mind about what the evils of opium can do to an individual; what it did to my uncle Reno, according to his brothers who revealed more detail than I could handle at the time. Keeping this image to myself, I picture him, along with other languorous smokers, as he cooks one lump after another, packs them into his bowl, inhales again and again, until his eyes glaze over while watching the smoke curl up to the ceiling. He passes into a trance, lying close to the other men and half-naked women flopped on wooden cots scattered about a sultry, cramped, filthy, cracked up opium den loaded with hookahs, and hats and coats hanging from fat, corroded nails pounded into vomit-smeared, pee-stained walls grown rust-colored, then black with years of smoke.

Had my other uncles read about this in letters? Had they seen some photographs? Or had they traveled to Chinatown in order to talk Reno into coming back home to Illinois?

There was this line from a book I once read about opium addiction: 'Like inside a sepulcher with the dead, no one speaks.'

A photograph on the next page showed a smoker with a stray eye. That man was holding a white cat who stared at the mouthpiece with more wisdom than anyone else in the den. He seemed to understand more about the destruction of humans than the humans did.

That life style went on until 1906, when the massive San Francisco earthquake, followed by fires, wiped out most of the opium dens, along with thousands of other buildings throughout the city.

Rubbing the side of my face, I tell the ladies what we learned after that: "There was a shutdown and public opium burning on Chinatown's streets in 1919, the same year Uncle Amer left our farm in Hadley to go homesteading. No one ever heard from Reno after that, did they?"

Hannah and Nellie glance at each other, gaze down at the ground, and shake their heads.

"I wonder," says Callie, "whatever became of him."

Shrugging my shoulders, I set my pipe down and sort through the rest of the envelopes lying next to me on the bench, in order to continue with Amer's story. The next letter I pull out is a favorite of mine. That is, except for the last paragraph; those lines troubled my family, gave us the first indication that things weren't going right for him.

April 20, 1919

Dear Vic, Julia, Will, and Ray,

I suppose you're wondering what it's like out here. I get good advice from John and other "honyockers" who have worked through several seasons of crops. I'll put in winter wheat come September. For now I'll plant a little corn and some oats. Don't think I'll go for the sugar beets, although a few of the farmers are trying them. The big crop out here, of course, is wheat. But there's some concern about severe drought conditions affecting everyone and causing low yields.

This yellowish soil isn't as rich and giving as the black loam I'm used to back home.

Every day, I follow my team through the fields. We don't finish turning sod 'til evening and then we're plenty tired by the time we head for the corral. The "boys" are pretty happy as soon as I pull off their harnesses and cool them down with a good brushing. They earn their feed every day, that's for sure.

I don't change out of my work clothes until after I've cut a few "bricks" to add to my shelter. I had to learn how to build a soddy or 'dobe, as some people call it out here. John helped me get started. I'm nearly finished, just need to rig up a window and locate a door. I've got my roof on—tarpaper over joists and topped with sod. Lumber is too expensive for more than the essentials, like ridgepole support for the ceiling.

I soak old newspapers and gather up mud and even a bit of horse dung for chinking all the holes. Mary had a few rags to spare for the purpose.

Every bit helps to seal out the wind. So you see, I'm getting lined up for winter a little every day. I'm told it gets pretty cold in these parts. But then I'm used to Minnesota winters, so I should be OK. My meals are mostly beef and boiled potatoes. Eager to taste a few early vegetables when the time comes. I'm getting along all right, though.

I don't keep up with washing my clothes like I should. I figure I'm going back into the fields come morning, so I hang my shirt and overalls on a nail next to the door frame, ready to go. By now, they might stand up in a corner all by themselves. Oh well, it's clean dirt, I tell myself.

Before bed I wind up the Victrola and play along while night settles in. Seems like my songs get swallowed up out here. I like to watch the late-working birds feed on what my plow turns over. It's as if they fly on the notes from my fiddle. Guess they approve. Radge runs his cuts and turns before settling down for the evening. You'd think he'd be tuckered out from following me around in the fields all day, but after supper he gets a fresh burst of energy and tries to herd the birds. You'd get a kick out of seeing him run free with a big grin on that long snout, stopping only to investigate a prairie dog hole.

I've met some good people, only there's one neighbor to the south by the name of Carmichael that's none too friendly. Doesn't seem to like my music. The other night I saw him ride his cow pony along the fence line that separates our land. He was looking out of sorts and whipping his horse's flank for no good reason that I could see. He gave me a stern look, then charged away. Didn't think my notes were that sour! Guess I'll have to practice some more.

With the last paragraph of that letter began our concern about Amer's safety. One of those uneasy feelings you try to shake off but can't. The following afternoon, he would give Tom Carmichael wide berth when he met up with him on the street of Jordan. The court records included this detailed testimonial from a witness:

Amer Lindstrom had just stepped onto the boardwalk in front of the post office when the confrontation took place. Tom Carmichael and his brothers, Jim and Seth, came on like schoolyard bullies, fanning out in front of Mr. Lindstrom.

Tom sneered and said, "Boys, I see a lily-liver comin' our way. What are we gonna do about that? With his hands at his sides, Mr. Lindstrom met their glances. He is a peaceful man from what I know of him. The Carmichaels, all large men, crowded and elbowed him off the boardwalk and onto the street. Then Tom pushed him down. I heard him tell Mr. Lindstrom that he had bet ter watch his back because "there'll be a next time."

This witness, a Mr. Johanssen, goes on to say there was no mistaking Tom Carmichael because of an unusual laugh that started deep in his throat and rose to a snarl. We learned that he had a penchant for shooting dogs roaming around the outskirts of town, and picking fights with honyockers, especially those who didn't blend in with the locals, or the first wave of settlers. They were a tough bunch, those Carmichaels—a trio of thugs.

I GET UP FROM MY BENCH to pass around a small black and white snapshot of Amer standing in front of his soddy, with Radge by his side.

"Oh, my," says Hannah, "look how his clothes hang on him. He must have lost a lot of weight."

Nellie leans over for a peek. "Is that his place? Why, those little buildings rise up so tiny against the sky. And such wide open land." She shivers. "It looks awful lonely out there."

"But see the way Amer is standing," says Cal, "with his feet planted wide and his shoulders back? He's waving—waving his hat at the sky."

I smile and nod at Callie. I've always liked this picture. After studying it for a moment—long enough to remember what it felt like to be there—I return to my bench and tuck the photo back into its envelope, shouting with pride, "Hell, he looks as if he owns Montana."

"Well, he looks dirt poor to me." Nellie crosses her arms. "And starving."

Like nearly everyone back then, Amer was pretty much broke, having spent all his savings on equipment and horses, everything it takes to get started with homesteading. And he never asked for help.

"In all that time," I say, twisting the packet string around my fingers, "he never asked for a thing—except once. And I'll get to that in a minute. First, I want to read from his next letter that, I'm sorry to say, contains the last of his high spirits."

May 22, 1919

> As busy as I am, these three years should sail by before my patent comes through. The work is hard but my horses and I make up a good team by now, almost come full circle after the spring planting and cultivating. They say the summers don't last long out here. I'm eager to put in my winter wheat. In past years, some of the farmers got as much as twenty-five bushels per acre. Isn't that something? We could use a little rain. No, a lot of rain. It doesn't look promising, but they say it will come. They're hoping for the same bumper yields as between 1910 and 1917. The war pushed the price up to $2.00 a bushel. It might even double. Imagine that!
>
> I rigged a fifty-gallon drum inside my soddy to burn kerosene when it gets cold. The railroad sells coal but it's too costly for my pocket. I use hay and swampgrass twisted into what they call "cats." That way it burns longer.
>
> I fixed up a shelf for my books out of scrap wood left over from the roof wedges. When the blizzards hit, Radge and the horses will keep me company, along with these books. Otherwise, I'll try to get over to the McKammans' now and again.

"See what I mean? Doesn't that sound hopeful? But the thing is, after that altercation in town, the Carmichaels became more cruel and aggressive, bored with dishing out more petty threats. When they couldn't get a rise out of Amer, they likely figured there was no way he'd give up and abandon his land. And that's when they came calling."

Chapter 6

The Hundred Dollar Smile

IT WAS NO SOCIAL CALL. Those Carmichael brothers—they were bad eggs.

I was struck by how Amer reported the attack, how he wrote it up in such detail. His affidavit reminded me of a script for a scene in some macabre play. Actually, the word "affidavit" sounds too formal when I think of those large, yellowed sheets of paper—a document completed in Amer's handwriting with the same brown ink and curlicues as on those letters he'd sent home to us. That original document had been attached to a typed version, filed in the sheriff's office, and used as evidence during the trial. Because of Amer's detailed testimony and what the McKammans told us about the night of July 14, 1919, I felt as if I'd been there. Witnessed the whole thing. Yet unable to ward it off.

Amer had just finished feeding Radge when the three Carmichaels—Tom, Seth, and Jim—rode up to the common gate on horseback. Amer might have gone along with Tom saying they just wanted to talk to him. But when one of the men made a belittling remark about extending an invitation for tea, Amer warned them not to come any closer—to stay off his land, period. The Carmichaels laughed and jeered, then charged in through the open gate and immediately surrounded him. They rode around Amer in a tight circle, telling him the land wasn't his and never

55

would be, that this was no place for the likes of him, and he should wise up and go back home where he belonged—back to that "milksop state" of Minnesota.

Amer edged toward his rifle propped against the soddy, but all three men slid off their horses and closed in on him before he could get to it. For some reason, he didn't have his revolver. The McKammans told us later on that he never wore it, that he usually left it inside his hut.

"This little guy needs some encouragin," Seth said, throwing a quick punch at Amer's face as if to tease him. Amer ducked and raised his fists in self-defense, but Jim and Seth grabbed him and pinned his arms. Tom doubled him over with a punch to the mid-section, then snapped his head back with a knee to the jaw. He spat on him and snarled, "If you knew what was good for ya, you'd pack up your fiddle and clear out! Your kind ain't welcome here."

He whacked him so hard with the butt of his pistol that Amer's teeth caved in like a handful of pebbles. Jim and Seth dropped him and he crumpled to the ground, bleeding from his mouth and nose. They'd broken his jaw and ruptured blood vessels around his stomach. Barking in a frenzy and showing his teeth, Radge lunged at the men. Before Amer passed out, he heard an awful yelp and caught sight of his dog flipping head over tail off Seth's boot.

It was dark when Amer came to. He lay on the ground for some time, then crawled inside his shelter and managed to wet a cloth for the swelling on his face. He heaved enough blood and tooth fragments to line the washbasin. Radge limped in and collapsed next to the bed. Amer was shocked and grateful to see him alive. If the Carmichaels hadn't already knocked the dog senseless, they might have shot him. Tom was most likely playing it smart so as not to attract the neighbors with the sound of a gunshot, especially from a revolver.

The following morning, John McKamman broke from work to check on Amer, concerned when he didn't see him in his field; for he was usually the first one out. Shocked by the bloody mess, he quickly bound the dog's ribcage, at Amer's insistence, then rushed my uncle into town to see the doctor and to file charges with the sheriff.

How we wished it had all stopped there. And that he could have received the protection he needed and deserved. To this day, I believe the law let him down.

This next letter, dated July 18, 1919, is the one that alarmed us—even though, as we learned later, it underplayed what really happened:

Now I don't want you to worry but some fellas got into a fight with me and beat me up pretty bad. They knocked out a big share of my teeth and I don't have the money for dentures and could use a little help. Once I get fixed up and put things to right on my place, I'll come back for a visit. I'm eager to see you and the folks in Hadley town. And the farm! I miss all of you. By the way, how's the corn? Suppose you laid it by some weeks ago. Be sure to keep an eye on it, boys!

I'll be all right. This business with my teeth and jaw set me back from getting at my work. I won't be scared off, though, from seeing my homestead title made official. I'm especially concerned for Radge. He'll recover, yet it'll take quite a while for his ribs to heal. The rest of him seems to be OK. He's pretty cautious, though, whenever he sees or hears someone approaching our land.

We hoped Amer would come back to Minnesota Johnny-on-the-spot. Mother and Dad rushed over to the bank in Hadley to borrow some money, which they wired to Uncle Amer, including a little extra for train fare. Their telegram urged him to be wary and to come home without delay.

At the time, we didn't know any details about what had brought on this attack. No idea who these people were or what they might do next. Was the law watching out for Amer? It didn't seem so. We were terribly anxious and eager to hear from him again. And so relieved when he sent this next letter, thanking us, grateful to begin the process of getting fitted for false teeth. That's when he finally revealed what was going on:

These fellas to the south, the Carmichael brothers, especially Tom, see me as an easy target. They're trying every way they can to jump my claim and scare me off the land.

I'm determined to hold on until my homestead papers come through. The headaches are pretty bad from these broken bones around my jaw and teeth. Hard to eat and keep up the strength I need for my fieldwork.

I notified the sheriff as to what happened. Not sure what more they can or will do, the sheriff and his deputy.

I'm eager to see all of you. And boys, you'd better get out there and dig some worms and rig up the fishing poles so we can catch a mess of bullheads over there at Lake Summit.

Meet me at the station in Pipestone. I'll be the man with the hundred-dollar smile!

Oh, boy, were we happy! Excited? We could hardly wait! Mother and Dad planned a big hoopla—delivered invitations, bought party favors, lined up our music, decorated the parlor with colored paper chains and stitched together a WELCOME HOME! banner that we draped along the wall above the piano. Mother even ordered a packaged assortment of balloons, "dye guaranteed not to rub off." It would be like welcoming Amer back from some foreign country, from the war, even.

Our kitchen smelled wonderful from all the food Mother was preparing: baked bread and mounded pies filled with slices of apples from last year's crop, roasting chickens and roast beef and pork. While she dressed out the game birds, Ray and I shelled peas and snapped the tips off string beans. Dad strung the last of our paper streamers above the dining room table.

In the middle of all this, there came a knock at the door. I jumped up to answer it, expecting to see a neighbor or Gus Block from the Hadley

Co-operative stopping by with extra butter. Instead, it was Mr. Byers, the wireless operator from town. He stepped inside the entry and stood for a long moment, somber, sad-eyed, reluctant to hand over the thin half sheet of pale yellow paper he'd drawn from his satchel. Across the top, in bold type, were the words "Western Union."

I felt the joyful energy of party preparations suddenly drain from my entire body. Legs and arms and hands felt numb, went limp as my mind raced to consider Mr. Byers' demeanor and what possible message that little piece of paper might contain. A clammy knot centered in my midsection, as if I'd just been punched. I called for Dad.

The three of us stood too close together in our narrow entry: Mr. Byers' back tight against the screen door; Dad and I facing that small sheet of paper, as if it were a firing squad. No one had to read the words. By the grim expression on Mr. Byers' face, we knew. There's a strange ambivalence that sets in when you're confronted with such a thing: You don't want to know. And at the same time, you need to know for certain what you already know.

With reluctance, my dad reached out and took it. Mr. Byers let go of the flimsy yellow sheet and slowly turned toward the door. "I'll wait outside for your reply, Vic," he said in a soft voice.

At times like that, everything alternately races and shifts to slow motion and you become aware of the minutest things: a dirt smudge on the entry wall; your father's work-worn fingers pinching the edge of a telegram, letting it hang at his side, reluctant to look at it; his bent back and sluggish movements as he manages the five steps back up to the kitchen.

Now, seventy years later, I can remember my own quick breaths and my father standing in the middle of our farmhouse kitchen, surrounded by colorful party favors and all that wonderful food, reading those few short lines on that Western Union telegram—silently at first. Then he looked up with the most wounded eyes I've ever seen on a man—stricken, physically, as if he had just taken an awful lashing—and read in a thin, raspy voice:

THIS IS TO INFORM YOU AMER LINDSTROM SHOT AND KILLED NEAR JORDAN MONTANA -(STOP)- BURIAL IN LOCAL CEMETERY UNLESS BODY CLAIMED WITHIN THREE DAYS -(STOP)- PLEASE ADVISE –(STOP)- BART FLEMING SHERIFF GARFIELD COUNTY

Mother and Ray froze where they stood, dumbfounded. Although I'd already had a bit of time to register its probable contents, the words on that little piece of paper hit me like an axe against a chopping block. Hard to fathom, when one minute you're in the middle of plans for a reunion party and the next. . . . Dad said nothing more for the longest time. He lowered his arm and let the telegram hang by his side while he gripped the edge of our cook stove, his face drained of color, his jaw set. He stared out of the window in the direction of the barn and the distant grove, sucking in quick, heavy breaths through his nose. That kitchen was so quiet you could hear the rhythmic whistling of Dad's breathing. Mother collapsed onto a chair and lifted her apron to her face. Ray began to cry. I felt like throwing up.

Since Amer's last letters, we'd had a bad feeling about "that Godforsaken country," as Mother called it. But this . . .

After a lengthy silence, Dad turned away from the window, laid the telegram on the table, cleared his throat, and spoke in a strained, yet determined, voice: "I won't have my brother buried like a pauper," he said, "unmarked and forgotten. We're bringing him home to Rockford."

From the hutch drawer he pulled out a tablet and a pencil and sat down to write. Ray and I moved aimlessly about the kitchen. When Dad finished, he got up and headed for the door. I followed him down the steps and outside. He thanked Mr. Byers for waiting, and handed him this reply:

ARRIVAL WITHIN THREE DAYS -(STOP)- PLEASE HOLD BODY AT UNDERTAKING PARLOR -(STOP)- VICTOR LINDSTROM

Mr. Byers, who knew and respected Amer, read the message, then paused, searching for his own words. He shook his head and placed his hand on Dad's shoulder.

"I'm sure sorry, Vic." Then he turned to me and said, "I'm awfully sorry, son. I know that Amer was like another father to you boys."

As far as I'm concerned, now that I'm an old man, the hardest thing a person has to do in life is turn his back on one who has just died. Turn his back, look over his shoulder, and walk away. Take care of the necessaries.

Almost as difficult is re-entering a house that shouts merriment and celebration when fate has played a mean trick, pulled the ace of spades from its sleeve, and left nothing to celebrate. As I've said before, it's at times like that when you notice the littlest things: a smooth gray pebble on the ground; crossed blades of quack grass at the edge of a path; a tuft of dog fur caught in the wire gate; the veins in a single maple leaf; oblivious chickens bustling about the farmyard; Fanny whinnying in the pasture. Then there was Bessie, resting her muzzle on the wooden fence, standing very still with a quizzical look, watching us plod up the steps to our door, as if she sensed something amiss. You see, she was Amer's favorite workhorse.

Inside our house, Ray scurried through the rooms like a little kid, tearing down paper streamers and bursting the balloons. He stomped on those that didn't break between his fingertips. No one stopped him. Afterward, he crumpled onto the floor, next to the piano.

Mother let the fire burn out in her cook stove and placed the meat and wild game in the icebox. I cleared the table and stacked the good dishes on the top shelf of the hutch. My father left the kitchen with telegram in hand. Gripping the long banister, he inched up the stairs like an invalid.

Later that evening, as the four of us sat around the dinner table, eating very little, Dad announced his plan. I suddenly felt older than my sixteen years when he told me that I was to go out west with him to claim the body.

"We'll leave first thing in the morning," he said. "And Ray, you're to stay with Mother. I need you to tend the farm while we're gone."

My brother looked stunned. "What! Why does Will get to go?"

No one replied at that moment. "I'm older than he is! I'm the one should go with you!"

"It's decided," Dad said in a quiet voice. Ray roughed his chair back from the table and jumped up, knocking over a glass of water. He ran to the door, yanked it open, and slammed it on his way out.

Mother got up to follow him.

"Let the boy be," said Dad, reaching for her arm. "He'll have to work through it on his own."

Mother did not sit down again. Instead, she stood at the window, watching, waiting. Then she dipped a washrag into a pan of water, wrung it out, and began wiping down the cook stove, all the while glancing out of the window.

Without being told, I knew why Dad had picked me to go with him to Montana. I felt proud, grown up, yet sorry for my brother. After that night, Ray and I were never again the same towards one another. I tried to be, but he cut me off, ignored me. From then on, we would pay a big price for Dad's decision, even though it was the right one.

Chapter 7

Indelible Mark

RAY SLEPT IN THE BARN that night and only returned to the house for breakfast the next morning. Mother had tiptoed out with a blanket and pillow, while Dad and I pored over the same railroad maps, timetables, and brochures that Amer had sent away for, then left on the bureau in his former upstairs bedroom. "I won't need these any longer," he'd said. "I'll soon be living the dream."

For me, the pictures of the Illinois Central and Great Northern had not only lost their luster, they seemed downright foreboding. The vegetation around the mountainside was brown and dry. And that charging black engine fronted with a cowcatcher no longer appeared inviting. Instead, it looked especially threatening, like a weapon, an outrageous barrel on some strange, gigantic shotgun.

The next morning, we drove directly to the train station in Pipestone and bought passage on The Great Northern, just as Amer had done months earlier. Like mourners next to an open grave, Mother and Ray stood at the edge of the platform several feet above the tracks, awaiting our departure.

As the train surged away from the terminal, I leaned out of an open window to look back at the other half of my family, wondering if I'd ever see them again. What were we getting into? Would we make it back alive? Mother blew a kiss and waved a handkerchief with her fingertips, as if she were shaking dust from it. Ray stood next to her, eyes downcast, fists jammed deep into his pockets. I realized then that my brother would never get the chance to say goodbye to Amer, never see him one last time. He and Mother would have to stay back to oversee the farm and tend the livestock, while Dad and I took the three-day journey into the unknown and another three days back again—a bitter adventure that would leave an indelible mark on my brother and me for the rest of our lives.

As the hours passed, jostled in our seats by the monotonous move-ment of the train, I tried to read my dad and look to him for a little com-fort. But there was none. From the blank look in his eyes to the little muscles around his mouth, I could detect no sign of emotion. After his initial reaction to the telegram, he simply withdrew into himself—his thoughts locked away, his face immoveable as stone.

I sat back and let myself be lulled by the swaying motion and rhyth-mic clickety-clack of the wheels. From my window, I mindlessly watched the comings and goings of green fields, pastures, fence lines, horses and cattle, clusters of sheep, shady groves, an occasional lake or slough. As the train slowed for crossings, it became easier to track the even rows of soybeans and tall corn. After a while the purpose of our journey and the hypnotic rhythm of the rails planted new words in my mind: Amer's wait-ing, Amer's wait-ing, Amer's wait-ing . . .

We stayed the first night in Granite Falls, then traveled for two more days and nights. At Miles City, we had to board the branch train to Forsyth. Dad had said next to nothing during the entire trip, except for a few passing comments in the dining car or in the sleeping car while dressing for bed. Each night, he honed his straight razor on the wide leather strop he'd brought along. Having been a barber in Rock-ford before moving to Hadley, he was meticulous and ritualistic, mak-ing sure his razor was sharpened for his next morning's shave. I sat on the top bunk in my pajamas, legs dangling over the edge, thinking up things to say. I guess I talked enough for both of us—about Amer and his land, about the men who had beaten, then murdered him. I created a dozen different scenarios for how he might have avoided getting killed:

"He should've practiced using his revolver and worn it in a holster at all times.

"He should have pressed charges after he was beaten up and insisted that the sheriff throw Tom Carmichael in jail.

"He should've gunned down those dirty varmints the minute they surrounded him, before they could lay a hand on him.

"He should have . . ."

Finally, Dad said, "Try to rest, son. We need to save our strength and our wits for when we get to Jordan."

After running out of words, I tricked myself into thinking that maybe, just maybe, there'd been a mistake. Someone else had been killed: a case of mistaken identity. Things like that could happen. Wouldn't it be something if my uncle were still alive? By golly, he'd be all right! He'll meet us at the station. Yes, by God, he'll be there to take us out to his land and show us the soddy he'd built and the fields he's going to plant in wheat. Dad and I will settle in, unpack, figure out where we'll sleep; Amer will have brought in a couple of extra cots for us, maybe. Or bedrolls laid out on the floor. Or we could sleep outside, next to a campfire; that would really be fun! Then we'll fuss over Sam and Rounder, Johnny and Skeeky, and brush and feed and water them. And Radge—I can't wait to run with that dog while he ushers up birds in the field. We'll all have a good laugh as soon as we see that wide grin on Radge's snout. "C'mon, Radge," I would shout, "let's race!"

"Good night, Will," said Dad in a soft voice, snapping my fantasy out of existence. "Get some sleep. Morning comes early."

During the last part of our journey into Montana, I whiled away the hours continuing to stare out of the window, making an effort to cast off the realization of what had happened to my uncle and the human element that had conspired to destroy him. Instead, I took in the landscape as Amer must have seen it from the beginning: the broad sun focusing on remarkable stone outcroppings, striking the faces of buttes, giving off shades of rose and mauve and ochre; banks of aspen and pines growing up from the valley, defining crevices and the twists and turns of the river.

The Yellowstone flows along the edge of town, in the opposite direction from where we were going. But the river wasn't as full and rushing as I thought it would be. In some places it presented itself as little more than a trickling creek. Then I remembered having heard about the terrible drought that had hit this area. As soon as we arrived in Forsyth, I saw just how low and yellow the water was, stained by the soil.

It was mid-morning of the third day when our train pulled into the Northern Pacific & Milwaukee terminal in Forsyth, Montana, an up-and-coming town with some of the most impressive houses and Main Street edifices I'd ever seen. I especially liked the Rosebud County Courthouse. Much later, I would learn that it had been built in 1914, just five years before Dad and I made the trip, twelve years after Rosebud was created from the western half of Custer County. It has always amazed me what human beings are capable of building once they set their minds to it: that courthouse, for instance, with its huge portico and octagonal tower topped by a copper dome.

His voice hinting at irony, Dad called it "The Glory of Forsyth."

And to think that not all that many years later, I would have an office inside "The Glory of Masterton," our Maywood County Courthouse, every bit as stately, with its own arched entry and bound ledgers (some dating back to 1887) tucked away in our vaults.

Dad and I collected our bags and stepped down onto the platform, uncertain what to do next or where to find transportation up to Jordan. The air was warm and dry. Some passengers set their luggage down on the dusty ground and rushed with open arms toward close friends or family. Others moved about deliberately, a few of the men stopping to check the time on their chained pocket watches.

"How will we get there?" I asked, feeling a bit apprehensive.

Dad looked around for a minute, then pointed off to the side, beyond the depot.

"I believe that fellow's for hire," he said, leading the way towards a man dressed in a long brown duster and tan driving cap, standing next to an impressive-looking vehicle.

I stopped in my tracks as soon as I spotted that fancy contraption—a four-door horseless carriage with mountainous wheelwells, mustard-colored, with seats in front, a bench behind, space for luggage, and a third row of seats. Two spare tires were strapped to the rear. I'd never before seen a car like it.

Dad rubbed a hand several times across his clean-shaven face. "I believe they call it a stage," he said.

"It doesn't look like any of the stagecoaches I've seen in movies."

"Course not," he answered. "I saw one once in a picture of our war generals riding in a car like that."

We approached the owner. Dad introduced himself, and me, shook hands, and said, "This is quite a vehicle."

Mr. Malloy, standing at attention, military-like, told us that he was indeed for hire, and suggested we head up to Jordan after taking our noon meal. But when Dad explained the urgency of our trip and what had happened to Uncle Amer, he agreed to start out immediately. We assured him that we'd eaten a filling breakfast on the train and were eager to get going. He and Dad settled on the price of a dollar a day.

I was relieved to meet the likes of Mr. Malloy, a man with a rough edge, but also somewhat compassionate—and familiar with the territory. At age sixteen, this was my first experience away from the farm, encountering plenty of moments when I felt that I'd been tossed into an uncertain world. Finding an ally, someone who'll stick by you in tough times, makes all the difference. I hoped Mr. Malloy would be able to help us from beginning to end—out of Forsyth, in to Jordan, and back again—and that nothing bad would happen to any of us.

While Mr. Malloy filled several canteens with fresh water from a fountain near the train station, Dad and I circled around the seven-passenger motorized Cadillac, admiring how it had been turned into the kind of vehicle that, free of dust, might have opened its doors to passengers dressed in tuxedos or smoking jackets, elegant trousers, spats, and a cane. Or to officers in uniforms with epaulettes and stars stitched onto their lapels. Mr. Malloy, in his sweeping duster and hat, never slouched while standing next to his stage.

We stowed our luggage in a space beneath the rolled up canvas that was used as a convertible top during inclement weather. Our driver got in and pumped up the fuel pressure by pushing and pulling on a rod to the right of the steering wheel. He turned the key to start the engine, adjusted the choke, and off we went in grand style—in an open touring car, just like General Pershing.

Because the day was hot and dry, we were able to cover the one hundred miles north to Jordan under a clear sky. And because we were the only passengers, we rode up front with Mr. Malloy, who sat ramrod straight behind the wheel.

As we motored through the main streets of Forsyth, he pointed out the Choisser Block, a wholesale liquor emporium, the Alexander Hotel, and the Forsyth Meat Market, housed in what used to be the Merchant's Bank; seeing the long links of sausages draped in the window made me hungry. After the courthouse, my favorite building was the Commercial Hotel, decorated in a diamond pattern with light and dark bricks, which we learned had been designed in the brickyard south of town. I was so taken with Forsyth and Mr. Malloy's narration that, for a minute, I almost forgot why we'd come to Montana.

Then a vision of Amer waiting for us at the undertaking parlor in Jordan hit me hard. If only my uncle had changed his mind and stayed in Forsyth. Yet, I couldn't imagine him working in a store or sitting behind a desk in some office. He was too much of a romantic and an outdoorsman for that. His goal in life was to become a homesteader.

The modern appearance of the bridge that would take us out of town surprised me. I had envisioned a rickety old wooden span, much like a railroad trestle. Mr. Malloy called the structure a "pin-connected through-truss bridge," explaining that the concrete piers and steel components had been fabricated in Pennsylvania, shipped by rail, then assembled and dedicated in 1905. "Hundreds of people," he boasted, "came to that dedication." Before the new bridge was erected, he said, Rosebud County residents had to ford the Yellowstone in low water, depend on irregular ferry service in high water, or travel forty-five miles parallel with the downstream to Miles City in order to get to the other side.

Inevitably, at frequent moments in our conversations, sadness and guilt came down on me like a heavy curtain, ending my brief enthusiasm for a bit of history, a beautiful building, a pretty girl walking down Main Street. We hadn't come to Montana for the sights, although it was pleasant to remember what Uncle Amer had written in one of his letters about the river and how it got its name: the Minnetaree Indians, first settlers, called it the Yellow Rock River. French trappers named it *Roche Jaune*, translated to "Yellowstone" by Lewis & Clark. *Roche* means rock, Amer contended, so why not call it that? Yellow Rock River.

And so, Mr. Malloy drove us across the through-truss bridge, leaving Forsyth and the low level of the Yellowstone behind. Thus began the final leg of our journey over the land of the Minnetaree, on the same dirt trail Amer had traveled months ago.

Near Jordan, Montana

Chapter 8

That Montana Sky

I THOUGHT SO HARD ABOUT my uncle during our passage from Forsyth to Jordan that I could picture him on the horizon, at the top of each little hillcrest; a lone man on a buckboard heaped with supplies, guiding four big horses into what would become The Badlands of Eastern Montana. I strained to hold him in my vision, until I could have sworn he was there, just ahead of us, and we would soon catch up with him. But it was only a mirage of the mind. And mirages, as everyone knows, are things you can never close in on.

With few intersections, the trail stretched as far as you could see and then some. In his letters, Amer called that road "a long brown ribbon, turned inky after dark." It was a difficult trail, rutty and bone-shaking. A few times I thought we'd rip out an axle. The ride was even bumpier because of the wheels—no such thing as inflatable rubber tires—and it made my young bones ache. It was to be a long trip. Night would fall before we reached Jordan.

Just then a wolf howled in the distance.

"A wolf cry at midday," said our driver, shaking his head. "Bad omen."

I shivered and glanced sideways at Mr. Malloy, waiting for him to explain. But he said nothing more about that wolf's cry. Just kept his eyes on the trail.

Besides his duster and hat, he wore leather driving gloves and goggles with barely a trace of dust on them. He was a good-natured sort with a ready smile, an abrupt manner, watchful brown eyes, and a side-arm. Guess you had to be tough to live out west, though he showed a different side when it came to his vehicle. Easing around potholes, he called her "My Jenny," and gave her little pats on the dashboard whenever the machine got us through a particularly rough section of road. During our rest stops, he wiped off the grime with one of several rags, and checked under the hood to see if she needed a drink or a little oil. He kept containers of gasoline, water, and clean oil on the floor next to the third seat, and repeatedly checked on those two spare tires lashed to the rear end.

"Taking proper care of my Jenny," he said, "can make the difference between life and death in this part of the country."

I didn't doubt him. Throughout the day, we never saw another soul on that dusty trail. So if he ever ran out of gas, motor oil, or water, and had no replacement for a broken tire, why then. . . .

"A wolf howling at midday, Mr. Malloy," I said. "Why is that a bad omen?"

"Signals a predicament. Wolves generally talk to each other early in the morning and at night. This one might mean a long separation from its pack or a fight over territory."

"Has any animal ever tried to chase you down," asked Dad, "making a trip like this?"

"Oh, no," he said, patting the dashboard again. "My Jenny here gets us through these crossings without so much as a nip at her hindquarters."

He laughed and sat up even straighter.

Mr. Malloy came to life whenever he talked about having such a modern conveyance for traveling across those great stretches of land that some folks called 'The Big Nothing.'

Dad had been right: that stage was the same model as those the government shipped to Europe for the war in 1917, used for staff cars and ambulances. In fact, Mr. Malloy's car had been in France during that time. It still had a bullet hole from a shot through the hood on the driver's side, next to the latch; it angled down steeply to the floor where a secondary hole had been patched. Mr. Malloy figured it had likely happened at the second or third Battle of the Marne, either from the air or by a shooter taking a bead on the driver. He'd left the outside bullet hole un-patched as a reminder of the Great War, but had painted over the entire olive-drab body until it acquired a shiny mustard tint.

The year before, on November 11, 1918, my friends and I had skipped school so we could march in an impromptu Armistice Day parade. I was fifteen years old then. What a coincidence that the very next year, I would imagine myself in a half-crouch position on the running board of Mr. Malloy's touring car, waving an M17 rifle, peering over my shoulder while our driver outran the Germans.

"General 'Black Jack' Pershing was very happy with his Cadillacs," explained Mr. Malloy. "They were fully armored with Colt machine guns for the fight against Pancho Villa, in the border war with Mexico. Many of the cars broke down, having no interchangeable parts. Even so, it was quite an advancement. You see, it was the first time in history that the United States fought a ground war using mechanized vehicles in place of some horses and mules.

And I don't know if you've ever heard about the 'Zimmerman Telegram.' Have you?" he asked, turning to look at each of us.

"No," said Dad.

"Back in February of 1917, the British intercepted an official German message sent to Mexico, proposing an alliance if the United States entered the war. The Germans would then aid Mexico in recovering Texas, Arizona, and New Mexico!"

"Wow!" I brought my hands up alongside my face.

"Less than two months later," said Mr. Malloy, "America declared war on Germany."

Wide-eyed and feeling patriotic, I might have enlisted right then and there in the middle of Montana's Badlands, picturing myself dressed in an army tunic, campaign hat, tapered trousers, brown boots with canvas leggings, a pistol in hand, tearing down to Mexico in that Cadillac rigged with machine guns, in search of Pancho Villa and his men. And maybe even some Germans.

"What else, Mr. Malloy?" I asked, eager for more information, glad to be focusing on other thoughts for the time being. "Why did they choose cars like this one?"

"General Pershing had a hunch, helped convince the government to run tests on them for two thousand miles across the Chihuahuan Desert, near Marfa, Texas. I'm pleased to report that not only did the touring car finish the test, it continued for another five thousand miles."

"Holy cow!" I said. "Imagine that! Five thousand more miles! Seven thousand miles total?"

"And that was in the heat of July, 1917." Mr. Malloy reached up to circle a hand in the air. "Turned out they only needed a thirty-cent fan spring and a gallon and a half of water."

"With that kind of record," said Dad, "I can see why they'd use them for the war effort."

Mr. Malloy wiped a tiny spot of grease off the steering wheel with his handkerchief. "Yep. Our government wasted no time shipping a fleet of these cars to France. So, have no fear. She will get you to Jordan and back."

Practically by the book, our driver knew everything there was to know about his 'Jenny' and her relatives. I looked at Dad, seated to my right. His profile and expression reminded me of a picture I'd seen of General Pershing in 1914, looking at once stern and sad. The General had just lost his wife and three young daughters in a fire at the Presidio in San Francisco. Only his little boy survived. How could anyone go on living after something like that?

For the six-year-old, I guess.

There we were in that big car with a flag holder soldered to the front and an unmistakable bullet hole in the hood, on our way to retrieve Uncle Amer's body, as if he'd been killed in the war. Except, his was a small war—over a land claim.

Or had Tom Carmichael murdered him for a different reason? Why would anyone kill another person over a piece of land? Especially when it wasn't all that productive. But that was war for you. Productive or not.

"Here in the West," continued Mr. Malloy, "these cars are, of course, far more comfortable than the old Concorde stagecoaches and six-horse teams from the 1800s. Those had to stop every ten miles or so, next to Little Porcupine Creek and Little Dry Creek, where there was water and grass for the horses, and food for the passengers. Though you had to be careful where you stopped in those days."

He'd heard of a woman by the name of Mrs. Corbet who planted herself in the middle of the trail, pointed her gun at a driver, and demanded that he pull over. Then she forced the passengers to eat meals at her table for one dollar per without any comment. That's how he put it—"one dollar per without any comment." He didn't know if she ever shot anyone, but heard she got to be very rich.

"Oh, Amer would sure get a kick out of that story," I said, imagining how exciting it would be to meet such folks along the way—as long as they didn't kill you.

Eventually, we did encounter one such odd duck at the halfway point: a grizzly old guy in filthy clothes, with sunken gray cheeks, bushy brown hair, and wary eyes, especially one. A yellow-gray beard hung down over the bib of his crusty overalls. Those whiskers were as matted and full of crud as unwashed fleece—a great wood tick hideout.

Packs of skinny dogs roamed around outside the shack. The old guy never got up from his chair, which was made from thick branches and sticks bent into shape and nailed together. It must have been a sturdy contraption, because he sat tilted back against a wall in the shade of an overhang, clutching a revolver on one knee and a bottle of whiskey on the other. I figure that whiskey is all he ever swallowed, because you couldn't drink the water in those parts—bitter as it was, tainted with alkali. Mr. Malloy warned us about a salty mineral that seeps through the soil and into the water. It smells bad too, as if other putrid stuff has seeped into it. Anyhow, the three of us drank soda pop fished from a large cooling box that hadn't seen ice in a long time. The inside was grimy with dirt and dried rodent carcasses, and we had to wipe coats of dust off the bottles before opening them. At least nothing had gotten into the soda pop; I downed mine in a few seconds.

You'd have thought the old man would be eager for company, but he never budged, except to set his whiskey bottle down on the ground so he could hold out a hand for our money. Never did hear the sound of his voice. Wonder if he even had one?

We decided to wait for other toilet facilities—a stop along the trail—because the pit behind that old guy's shack was so foul you couldn't get within ten feet of it without gagging. I was glad to get out of there and back into our car. It took a good mile in the open air before that stench cleared from my olfactories. To this day, I can conjure up those awful smells—not that I care to—and that place, which comes to me in shades of tanned leather and dried cornstalks. In my mind that old geezer sits propped against a splintered wall, swilling his brew, gun at the ready, until such time as he drops over dead. For all I know he and his dogs are still there, gone to dust and skeletons next to the remnants of that old stick chair—nothing left but empty whiskey bottles, a gun, and piles of bones.

"I've been by there any number of times," said Mr. Malloy, "and the old codger never shows the slightest indication that he recognizes me. Ekes out a living the only way he knows how. Probably started out kinda hopeful, just like those sodbusters who thought the land would provide everything they'd planned for as soon as it went under the plow. And the weather would behave itself. Problem was they weren't only farmers from your neck of the woods—men who started out with some sense. It was a bunch of clerks and barbers and factory hands from the east that came out here in droves, thought they were getting a good deal. Three things they didn't know sic 'em about: building a shelter, knowing where and how to find water, and gathering fuel to keep from freezing to death." Mr. Malloy waved an arm toward the land. "No logs on the plains, as you can see. A bunch of those people ended up burning their fence posts and furniture. Not many streams, either. If they didn't starve or freeze to death or break down from their labor, they died from the prairie fever."

"What's that?" I asked.

"Typhoid—from drinking bad water. Some folks got so desperate, they resorted to collecting what little water they could find in shallow buffalo wallows."

"Well, my brother started out right," said Dad. "He built his soddy and dug a well, first thing."

"That's the only way," said Mr. Malloy. "You got to know this part of Montana, extremes in the weather. Nature was good to us until 1917. It rained aplenty and wheat soared to two dollars a bushel on account of the war. We got twenty-five bushels to the acre back then. Best in the entire country. Our 'Wheat Miracle Year' was 1915. We provided forty-two million bushels for a war to end all wars—enough food to win the war.

"But the wet years end and the dry ones come. And along with that, hardships no man can predict—like going down to two or three bushels per acre. When things like that happen, there's always some know-it-all member of an agricultural committee who minimizes conditions and attributes the whole affair to honyocker inexperience."

"Any idea as to how many homesteaders came in over these past few years?" asked Dad.

"I'm not sure of the number, but I heard that by 1910, million of acres had been taken up here in Montana. Quite a few of the settlers left, though—starting around 1917, on account of the drought.

"A wind'll blow 'til the land parches and cracks. Not much grass left to hold the soil. Too many plows have seen to that. We might have to submit a bill to North Dakota for all the topsoil that blows in there from Montana." Mr. Malloy smiled and winked with that comment. "I remember reading a few rhyming words in our local paper a while back: 'Twenty miles from water, forty miles from wood. We're leaving old Montana, and we're leaving for good.' Desperate folks, those homesteaders."

I wondered if Uncle Amer was able to get his share of acreage for cheaper, but didn't bother to ask. Not only did it not matter anymore, I was very much taken by all that Mr. Malloy had to talk about.

"We're already seeing buildings banked with tumble weeds," he added. "You think there's rain in a summer cloud. Look again. Might be hail.

I'd say this area is ripe for disaster. We'll just have to wait and see what 1920 brings."

The dark started closing in on us like a shroud, and the land looked like a big lonely nothing with the bleached bones of animal carcasses scattered about. The trail was just as Amer had described it in one of his letters: "a long black ribbon, eerie in the dark, but also one of the most beautiful places I have ever seen."

Despite all the negative stuff I'd heard about "major losses for honyockers," I felt connected to my uncle that night. As soon as the darkness came down, blacker than black, Montana's huge sky exploded with stars, and the horns on grazing steers shone a pearly white in the starlight.

Mr. Malloy slowed down, stopped the car, and turned off the headlights, which, for a brief moment, had caught a mule deer and a few smaller night creatures scurrying off and away. There we were, beneath the same brilliant firmament Amer had loved—a deep, wide sky strung with jewels, like fireworks that never fizzle out.

We stepped down from the stage and stood for a moment at the edge of our trail. Mr. Malloy invited us to follow him several yards away from the car and onto the uneven prairieland. He spread his arms wide and looked up at the sky.

"Nowhere," he said, "except maybe at sea, do you get this kind of elbow room."

He was right. The sky came down all around at the same distance. We stood there like three small pins on a gigantic map.

"Got to respect it, though. Just like the sea, you don't ever take it for granted. My wife and I took a trip to the Big Snowy Mountains near Lewiston: Greathouse Peak. It's beautiful, of course, but those mountains swallowed us up. Can't imagine living in the Rockies, unable to witness an early sunrise or a late sunset.

"A man from eastern Montana, well, he feels hemmed in amongst the peaks. I needed to come back home, spread out, and smell the sage."

We sniffed at the air and sure enough, you could have rubbed some big Thanksgiving turkeys with the scent that night.

Our time in Montana, away from city lights, is something that has stayed with me, even into old age. Years ago, when I walked the streets of Masterton in winter, and Callie and I visited Mother every Tuesday evening, I thought of that Montana sky and those zillions of stars, as Cal would call them. It was a part of Amer's vision. His dream. Gave him a lift, a sense of calm during the short time he lived. As I've often said, it's good for the soul to be at one with the out-of-doors. Makes a fellow feel alive, larger than himself. That's what actor William Holden said about his time spent in Africa; that it distances one from the foolish, petty bickering that goes on in the world of people. And I learned from Mr. Malloy that one should never slough off and destroy our natural surroundings. Instead, we must prepare for living in and with them. And learn from them.

"Respect," he said. "Accept and respect."

WE ARRIVED IN JORDAN late that evening, logy and disheveled from our three days of travel, including those one hundred miles through the great prairie land. The town was larger and more populated than I thought it would be—over 2,000 souls. Mr. Malloy explained how it had grown because of the Homestead Boom that began around 1910.

Along either side of the main thoroughfare—a dirt street edged with raised boardwalks—white clapboard buildings stood out in the dark. Our headlights illuminated storefronts and boardinghouses. It was late and not many people were out. The only sounds above our motor were faint music from one of the saloons, a couple of young boys calling out to one another, and a few barks from a black and white herding dog trotting along the boardwalk, parallel with us. Dust raised by our car hung in the air for a moment as soon as Mr. Malloy pulled over and stopped in front of the jailhouse.

"I'll wait for you back at the hotel while you talk to the sheriff," he said, indicating one of the white buildings that we'd passed, about two blocks away.

The boardwalk stopped several yards before the jail, which was located at the far end of town and a half block off Jordan's Main Street. It was a solid, square building with a flat roof and an arched addition, stout as a fort with weeds growing up against the patchy concrete foundation. Nearby stood a monstrous dead tree, lopsided, tilting like a giant scarecrow without clothes, planted as if to scare off intruders; it reminded me of a hanging tree.

The Jordan jailhouse

Built of brick and mortar, the jailhouse was smudged in large sections with graying cement, some of which had pealed away to reveal the rusty red shades of bricks. A slab in front seemed to lead up to a door, but there was none—only a small barred window. Unsure how to get inside, we circled the entire structure a couple of times, shuffling along in the dark. Through a second barred window in the back, we could see the flame from an oil lamp flickering inside. Where was the entry?

Sheriff Fleming, who had sent us the telegram about Uncle Amer, evidently saw us nosing around. He stepped out of an obscure rear door, right fingers placed against his holster. As soon as Dad spoke up and the sheriff realized who we were, he held out his hand to shake ours, and invited us inside.

Fleming was a gruff, no-nonsense fellow with bristly eyebrows and a thick white mustache. It was obvious that over the years he'd faced off with a lot of rough men. And weather, which had tanned and toughened his skin. Pinned to his brown vest was a large silver badge—a six-pronged star, imprinted with fancy letters that spelled out the word "Sheriff."

Now that we'd finally made it to Jordan, I wondered how Dad was going to handle things. Under the light of a hanging lantern, he looked all tuckered out, hesitant to speak up. Ever since that telegram had made its way into our farmhouse back in Hadley, he'd been extremely quiet and seemingly played out.

Standing inside this jailhouse and witnessing Dad's reluctance to speak up, then hearing him struggle to say what might have been on his mind, disappointed me, made me nervous and afraid. But the sheriff said he'd been expecting us and motioned for us to sit down in a pair of sturdy chairs next to his desk. He expressed his condolences with a few clipped words, then got down to business, as if dealing with Amer's murder was all in a day's work.

"From the evidence," he said, "your brother was shot with a .45 caliber Colt automatic. It was Tom's gun, all right—a U.S. Army model. My deputy found it on Carmichael's land, hidden in a prairie dog hole."

Just then, we heard a loud, gravelly voice from another part of the jailhouse: "Hey! Hey, out there. Self-defense. It was self-defense!"

With a sneer, Sheriff Fleming muttered, "Not likely."

He stood and clomped over to a connecting door and hollered, "Shut up in there, Tom, or you won't get breakfast in the morning. Now, shut the hell up!"

Dad was staring at the sheriff with wide eyes, bloodshot from lack of sleep.

"What's going on?" I whispered, feeling frightened. Dad shook his head.

Here we were just steps away from the man who had murdered Amer. There shouldn't even be a trial, I thought. He should be lynched right now. I'll help string him up on that tree outside. But that's not how the system works, unless a mob takes over. Nevertheless, it was an insult to have to be in the same building with this killer. And taken in by a sheriff who seemed to grow less sympathetic around us as the seconds hammered by on the Seth Thomas wall clock. Tick-tock, tick-tock.

Returning to his desk, Sheriff Fleming announced that Tom would remain locked up until his trial, which hadn't been slated yet, and that the deputy would attempt to keep a close watch on the other two Carmichael brothers.

"They've been hanging around town," he drawled, "stirring up trouble, trying to garner support for Tom. They shouldn't bother you none. I don't think they know you're in town. Leastwise, I hope not. We sure as hell don't need any more Easterners getting themselves shot around here."

I bristled at the sheriff's comments and at his nonchalant attitude. Scooting forward in my chair, I opened my mouth to speak. If Dad wasn't going to assert himself, then I would. But before I could call out the word "Midwesterners," my father gently placed a hand on my arm.

"We want to see my brother," he said softly. "And locate his land."

The sheriff reached for an Eversharp and a tattered black record book, opened it to one of many pages filled with names and numbers, and penciled some figures he found onto a scrap of paper.

"His claim," he said, "is located two miles north of town; section forty-aught-thirty-three, acreage 251101 PA. You'll find those numbers on the stakes. Range 035 is where the shooting took place."

Dad thanked him—too kindly, I thought. But then he made up for everything as soon as he rose from the chair. In spite of his exhaustion, he stood up straight and said, "My brother was a good man, Mr. Fleming, a hard worker. Prepared for what he needed to do as a homesteader. He came here to farm, not to get killed."

"Yes, well . . . I'm sorry," said the sheriff, ushering us out the door and pointing in the direction of the boardwalk. "You'll find the undertaking parlor yonder, past the hotel, inside one of those fancier white-frame build-ings at the other end of town. Not very convenient," he snorted, "especially when a prisoner decides to hang himself here in his cell." He chuckled and adjusted his cowboy hat. "At least it saves on the cost of a trial. Anyhow, Undertaker Henry Hawkins is expecting you first thing in the morning."

Eager to get out of that jailhouse, I quickly edged away from the door and scooted toward the hanging tree. Dad was close behind.

"By the way," called out Sheriff Fleming, "you might want to talk to the McKammans. They were good friends of your brother. The mis-sus was with him when he died. In the meantime, we'll keep an eye on things here in town."

As we headed in the direction of the hotel, Dad checked his pocket watch. "Ten o'clock," he said, with a slight choking sound. "It's been a long day."

"Three long days," I reminded him. Still aggravated by the chilling exchange with the sheriff, I added, "That guy should have kept an eye on things before Amer was killed."

Dad clenched his jaw. "I know, son. I agree."

In the sultry night, we moved along through stretches of dirt and clumps of grass before reaching the boardwalk. Most buildings on Main Street were dark, except for two saloons and a dim light inside the hotel.

Oh, what comfort it was to find our driver sitting on a bench out front, watching and waiting for us. After meeting with the sheriff, it was especially heartening to see Mr. Malloy's friendly face again. He stood up and smiled, then clapped a hand on each of our shoulders as we made for the door.

Like many of the buildings in town, the hotel consisted of a white-frame structure, narrow with three stories. It appeared to include no more than a half dozen rooms, since the lobby and dining room took up the first floor. The gloomy check-in area smelled musty and moldy, as if accumulated rainwater had seeped in during the wet years and never completely dried.

Behind a chest-high, gummy wooden counter sat the desk clerk, a puny fellow with round glasses and thin yellowish hair. Not a very likeable sort, to my way of thinking. Seemed like one of those high-strung, self-important busybodies with nothing worthwhile to back up his patter. Apparently adept at reading the hotel register upside-down, he got all excited over our signatures—hands a-flutter as he placed the pen in its holder and capped the inkwell. His voice pitched up an octave and his words came out in staccato.

"Tom Carmichael's brothers are in town," he chattered, waving a copy of the Jordan Gazette under our noses. "But Sheriff Fleming and his deputy are watchin' 'em real close. They've got Tom in jail. I don't think you need to worry none. All the same, I'd watch my back if I was you. There could be real trouble. I hear talk of a vigilante committee. Yes, sir, real trouble."

His comments sounded rehearsed, as if he'd been gossiping for days with everyone who came in. He seemed to be the type who itched to see a shoot-out on Main Street.

"We'll be fine," Dad told him in his usual slow, calm voice. "All we need is a good night's sleep and a warm breakfast in the morning."

The clerk sniffed and tossed his head. "Rooms around back," he said brusquely. "Up one flight. Breakfast at six."

One of several things I was learning about my dad, made clearer by his exchanges with the sheriff and now the desk clerk, was that he knew how to handle all types with as little fuss as possible. His unruffled attitude reminded me of the placid waters in our pond back home.

Dad and I, along with Mr. Malloy, carried our bags back outside and threaded our way through the dark in order to locate the rear staircase, the only way we could get to our rooms. As we started up the steep plank steps, we found that three of them were missing, plus there were no backings on those steps, and no railings to hold onto. Not even a tipsy one. We finally made it to the top and in through a small door to the narrow second floor hallway.

Dad had to light a match to see the numbers on the doors. Mr. Malloy's room was directly across from ours. Before turning in for the night, we thanked him heartily for all he had done to help us get through this day.

"We couldn't have managed without you," said Dad.

Jordan Hotel

Accepting our thanks, Mr. Malloy said he'd see us at breakfast and would be glad to stick around while we went to the undertaking parlor.

"And I'll drive you out to Amer's place afterward," he said, shaking our hands. "I'd like to see you through."

"We're mighty grateful," said Dad.

And were we ever. And was I ever! Dad and I had each other, but he'd been so quiet during all that time on the train and in the stage, I often felt as if I were making the trip alone. Although his brief exchanges with the sheriff and the hotelkeeper gave me a little more confidence, having someone like Mr. Malloy stand by us meant everything. He knew what life was like in that part of the country.

Chapter 9

Sagebrush Before the Wind

OUR HOTEL ROOM, large and sparsely furnished, was the size of a wing in an old dance hall. Not that I'd ever been inside one before. But I could imagine floozies and dandies taking a break from their strenuous exercise, fanning themselves, standing around, having a smoke and a drink next to this wall or that wall.

In our room, the high ceiling and a scuffed wooden floor seemed to slant off-level in opposing directions. The dark floral print wallpaper refused to brighten when I lit the oil lamp on a small table next to the bed; partially because there wasn't much wick left. The rest of the room's décor consisted of a washstand with a white pitcher etched all around by tiny dark cracks, a matching basin, one dingy gray washcloth, and a faded blue hand towel. The water in the pitcher appeared thick with its filmy surface glancing up at me.

On the floor, beneath the high metal-framed bed, sat an old white "thunder mug," as Uncle Amer used to call each of our chamber pots at home. It was a relief to know that we wouldn't have to go back outside in the dark and maneuver those tricky steps in order to find an outhouse.

Stripped down to our underwear, Dad and I took turns scrubbing ourselves with a sliver of soap and chilly water poured from the pitcher into the basin. Then we flopped down onto a lumpy mattress that was barely wide enough for one hefty man. Fortunately, we were both thin.

It was hard to settle in for the night. Strange noises came from a room down the hall, a sort of bumping sound, like someone moving furniture. Our mattress was not only lumpy, but sagged toward the floor on my side.

Within minutes, we jumped up with a shout, yanked the musty sheets off the bed, and hustled through the door to shake them out over the roof's edge. Bed bugs.

Not that it did much good, shaking off those covers. We wondered if Mr. Malloy was experiencing a similar problem.

After remaking the bed, we lay there in the dark, scratching and talking some more about Amer and the Carmichaels. I told Dad that he should buy a gun first thing in the morning. He quietly chuckled, said he didn't think we'd need one, and turned over on his side to face the wall. His laugh had a bitter edge to it.

I started feeling pretty much alone again.

All kinds of images worked my brain that night: I wondered about the mortuary and what Amer would look like dead. Where on his body had he been shot? I'd never seen a human corpse before—only animals, on the farm, along with those we'd hunted. It made me feel panicky if I thought about my uncle like that for too long. I forced my thoughts to picturing Tom Carmichael pacing inside his cell at the county jail, yammering away like when we were there. Would the sheriff withhold his breakfast in the morning? Or maybe the murderer had fallen fast asleep, with no remorse.

His brothers weren't implicated, but they'd been hanging around town, acting tough, talking big. That is, if we could believe the hotel-keeper. The town seemed as dark and foreboding as a cave when you have no idea what or who might be lurking deep inside. And just as quiet. After the saloons closed their doors for the night, that silence began to unsettle me. The town seemed like a powder keg.

I gently poked Dad in the shoulder, because the more I thought about our situation, the more I figured we ought to have a gun.

Half awake and groggy, he said, "It might make matters worse, son. Try not to worry. We have no choice but to trust that the sheriff and his deputy will be looking out for us."

"Yeah," I muttered for the second time that night. "The way they looked out for Amer."

I could sense Dad fully awake as he rolled over onto his back again and stared up at the ceiling until the oil lamp fizzled out. "I know, Willie," he said quietly. "They didn't do right by him."

Then my father said another thing that has stuck with me ever since; a lesson that will stay with me 'til the day I stretch out for good. Dad was never one to go on at any great length about matters, but that night he gave me a rare piece of advice that shed light on how he had dealt with the sheriff and the hotelkeeper: "No matter what the situation, Willie," he said, "no matter what confronts you in life, try to do what you have to do in a dignified way."

Then he turned onto his side, faced the wall again, and told me to get some sleep, because we were going to face a rough day tomorrow.

I relaxed as best I could, feeling a bit more confident that Dad would be able to deal with the undertaker the next morning—whatever that man's demeanor.

More important was how my father would react to the sight of his brother. And how would I?

Seems like I'd just dozed off when it was time to get up. Dad and I took turns using the "thunder mug," then scrubbed our faces in the last bit of cold, scummy water from the pitcher before dressing for breakfast.

Each of us had packed two changes of clothing: socks, good trousers, underwear, and shirts. Mother had pressed everything, even our socks and underwear. You could still catch the faint whiff of her hot iron on wind-dried cloth. I was cheered by changing into clean clothes after all that time on the train and in the stage. How little it takes, sometimes, to comfort a fellow in a tough situation. For me, it was knowing that we still had a set of fresh clothing, pressed and folded by Mother, for our return trip home.

In addition, it was refreshing to step outside and breathe in that early morning air, exhilarating to see Jordan at daybreak with its bustle of people moving along the boardwalks on either side of a hard-packed Main Street. The town didn't seem as threatening in the new light as it did in the dark of night. The front of our hotel looked welcoming, painted white with pale green trim and the name Jordan Hotel lettered in black across the top like a billboard.

Daylight provided us with a panorama of this boomtown, the Garfield county seat: hotel, general store, lumber mill, post office, rooming houses and two saloons. At the far end, beyond the jailhouse, a blacksmith shop stood next door to a livery stable. I never took much notice of those buildings the night before, when all I was willing to see was the "hanging tree." And then I spotted a couple of dogs leaping across the narrow creek and onto open land.

Several children with neatly combed hair were skipping along the street toward a sod structure called Vail Creek School, located on the outskirts of town. Girls in middy dresses and boys wearing short pants and jackets carried lunch pails, strapped books, and wrapped presents. But it was July, and I wondered why they were heading off to school.

What is it about the light of day? No matter where you are in the world, when things are at their bleakest, and you feel like you're starving in more ways than one, good old Sol, a row of bright buildings, lively children on their way to a birthday party for their teacher, and a greeting or two from strangers work wonders; neutralizers that help chase away the dread. Even though we had yet to meet with the mortician and view Amer's body, my concern for our own safety—and the near-desperate uncertainty I'd felt in the middle of the night inside that dark, bed-bugged hotel room—waned, edged out by a clear sky and the promise of sunshine. And the delicious smells of breakfast cooking.

Mr. Malloy was already inside the dining room, visiting with another hotel guest and several ranchers whose horses we'd noticed while easing down the rear steps from our hotel room and circling around to the main entry. A few more cowboys rode up, dismounted, and tied off their reins at the hitching rails where a long row of patient chestnut, black, paint, and buckskin horses stood shoulder-to-shoulder, with a hint of fresh trail dust coating their hindquarters.

Boots clomped on the boardwalk and spurs jingled as a dozen men, including farmers and ranchers, joined us in the dining room that morning. Word had gotten out that Amer Lindstrom's kin had arrived from Minnesota.

With somber nods, they shook our hands and removed their hats, as if at a funeral visitation. Then we all sat down together at a large oblong table and waited for our food.

Breakfast was served family style: platters heaped with thick slices of roast pork and beef; slippery stacks of fried eggs, sunny side up; large bowls of steaming potatoes, gravy and pork drippings; mounds of buttered biscuits; pails of hot coffee. The food was good, but I didn't have as much of an appetite as I thought I would, as I felt through the night and out on the boardwalk. It just didn't seem right to be sitting at a table among all those men, without Amer. No place setting for Uncle Amer. That he should be lying inside the mortuary a short distance down the street from us, four days dead, was . . . well, I couldn't find a word for the awful feeling it gave me.

A glance around the table made it obvious which of the men likely had a wife or sister at home. Or a mother. Those were the scrubbed ones with trimmed hair, clean clothes, and a fresh bandanna around the neck. The rest all seemed the same—lean, grim, sun-burnt, except for their foreheads, dull-eyed, worn out. A couple of them had the look of men who'd lost too many spring crops to large hail. I've seen plenty of those types over the years—farmers forced to stand by, helpless, while their young corn plants got shredded and beaten to the ground. After all those weeks of labor. I never saw them give up, though—those farmers.

Unsmiling, solemn, but steady, they always returned to their fields the next day, ready to replant.

Against the quiet, you could hear several horses nickering at their hitching posts. The soft clatter of breakfast dishes and the occasional shuffling of boots beneath the table were the only sounds inside.

These men had ridden in that morning out of curiosity, but they were also there to pay their respects and to tell us what they knew about Amer and about the Carmichaels. You could sense their tacit sympathy. When they finally spoke, it was with an abruptness similar to Mr. Malloy's.

Half way through our meal, one of the men started up about how a Homestead fight affected everyone, made them all jittery. Then, one after another, each man had his say:

"The Carmichaels don't like fences. And they don't like cattle."

"You interfere with the way they see fit to running things, they'll come after you."

"Mean cusses, especially Tom. Just as soon shoot you as look at you."

"They have a reputation around here for letting their sheep graze everybody out."

"That's for sure. Those assholes drift with their stock and when one section is used up, they move on to the next. Hell, they don't give a damn whose land it is."

"About your brother, Mr. Lindstrom," said one with thin, cigarette-scarred lips, "it was more than a Homestead fight. It got personal."

"Personal?" said another, shaking his head. "I don't know . . ."

"Hell, yes. There was no doubt where the stakes were on Amer's claim. I'll say it again—it got personal."

"I think that's true," said a rancher with worried eyes and deep creases at the corners. "He tried to stand up to Tom, but he . . . You see, out here, some folks pick on them that's soft."

"He wasn't one to take hard liquor—your brother. Other'n that, he was an all right sort of fella."

A few of the men chuckled over that comment.

"All I can say is we've had enough of them Carmichael grifters, especially Tom. I'd sure as hell like to get on that jury. Just as soon see him hang, that son of bitch."

As quickly as those men started talking, they fell quiet, everything of importance having been said. With gnarled hands, they ate the rest of their meal in silence. The only sound left was the scraping of flatware against crockery.

Those last spoken words lingered in my mind: "Just as soon see him hang. . . ."

For a second, I pictured a faceless man with a noose around his neck, dangling from that "hanging tree" next to the jailhouse.

Dad and I had learned more from those locals and settlers at breakfast than from Sheriff Fleming the night before. Had Carmichael really accused Amer of claiming a portion of land that he, Carmichael, said was rightfully his? Or was there more to it? Why hadn't the sheriff told us any of this? Moreover, why hadn't my dad asked questions?

What troubled me was the notion of Amer being called soft. He was a gentleman, true, but he could stand up for himself when he had to. I never took him for a pushover. He was a crack shooter at trap. And he pitched a hell of a game for the Hadley Buttermakers. What was the real reason for his murder? And why hadn't the law stepped in—especially after that awful beating?

When it came time for our appointment with the undertaker, Dad stood and thanked everyone for joining us and for their kind words about Amer. Before leaving the dining room, I took one last look at the gaunt, sinewy builds of those ranchers and farmers, their finger-combed hair, pale brows, and powerful work-worn hands.

They all glanced up at us and paused as we turned to go.

Without expecting an answer, one said, "Will we ever see his like again?"

Then they sent us on our way with quick nods, timeworn eyes, and went back to the task at hand—mopping up egg yolk with chunks of biscuit.

Outside of the hotel, we had to stop on the boardwalk and shield our faces from a sudden gust that whipped up small brush and clouds of dust. A whirl of wind put on quite a show, spinning and dancing the length of Main Street, chasing down brittle brown tumbleweeds, bowling them from one end of town to the other.

"Sagebrush before the wind," said Dad, peeking around the edge of his coat collar held up against his eyes.

Those words carried a double significance that day. Long ago, he used them to describe his four brothers and himself, abandoned by their father, orphaned by the deaths of their mother and sister:

"We all went our separate ways," he used to say, "comin' and goin', like sagebrush before the wind."

Chapter 10

It's Only the Shell, Willie

OUR PATH TO THE UNDERTAKING PARLOR was not a smooth one. Half way along the boardwalk, we came upon two rough-looking men slouched on a bench in front of the General Store. I knew right away who they were.

Those thugs didn't even have to utter a word—their surly, rotten attitudes showed through by the way they sat and the way they glared at us. Hooligans. Up to no good. Dad and I slowed our pace. Just like in an old western shoot-'em-up, we witnessed some rotters ready to stir up trouble. And then we spotted the sheriff, on the other side of the street; he was leaning against a hitching post, arms folded across his chest, trying to look nonchalant. As soon as Sheriff Fleming saw that we were aware of his presence, he reached up and pushed the brim of his Stetson back with his thumb.

The Carmichael brothers sneered and stared at us with expressions as wicked as a man can conjure this side of Hell. Their teeth resembled yellowed Chiclets poking out of leathery faces the color of beef jerky, topped off with filthy cowboy hats. I checked their sides for guns, but didn't see any holsters. Who knew? They might have concealed Derringers or Bowie knives inside their boots. One of them stretched his arms wide, yawned, and stuck his long legs straight out, forcing us to sidestep.

I stopped and looked the guy full in the face. Mean? I have never in my life seen eyes like his—onyx hard, like a snake's. I didn't know which brother I was staring down, Seth or Jim, but I felt like spitting on his dusty old boots. He stood up and slowly came toward me, clenching his fists and pinning me with the look of a baited bull.

"Somethin' ailing you, kid?" he said, spitting tobacco juice on the boardwalk next to my feet.

Halfway hypnotized, I stared back, speechless, blind to the chance I was taking by standing there with my hands on my hips and as dirty a look on my face as I could toss him. Suddenly, that bully flipped the bird at me and started to hiss between black-brown teeth.

Before I could flick my own finger, the sheriff called out and started running down the street in our direction. The roughneck stopped hissing and tensed up, shifting his attention between us and the sheriff, while his brother, still seated on the bench, reached down to tug at his pant leg.

Dad grabbed hold of my arm and quickly steered me along the boardwalk, away from the two Carmichaels.

"Stay calm, Willie," he whispered as we hustled along, "don't show any fear."

But I was more angry than afraid—and a bit cocky; natural, I'd say, for a sixteen-year-old. I turned and nailed that guy with the fiercest look I could muster, focusing on his beak of a nose instead of those snake eyes. The sheriff approached them with a shout, "Hold it right there, Jim!"

Seconds later, a shot rang out! Hunkering down, with hearts racing, Dad and I scurried behind the post office. Dogs barked. A woman screamed and darted past us. After a minute of dead silence, we peeked around the corner.

Jim Carmichael, up from the bench with his hands raised, had evidently tried reaching into his boot. The sheriff handcuffed both men and hustled them off to jail.

Sheriff Fleming had called out the warning and fired his revolver, presumably in the air.

My heart pounded for a long time after that.

"OH, WILLIAM!" CRIES HANNAH, edging forward on her bench. "That was an awful chance you took! Why, just imagine, you and Vic might have been shot on your way to the mortuary. Oh, dear Lord. . . ."

Nellie fans her face with an old church bulletin dug out of her purse. "I can't even begin to think of something like that happening here in Rockford," she says, her upper lip beading with sweat.

"Or back home in Minnesota," says Cal. "Can you picture a shoot-out on Masterton's Main Street?"

That question brought back the memory of a man who had killed his wife and mother-in-law, not on Main Street, but smack-dab in front of the Catholic Church, a half block from our house. Unarmed, of course, those women were dressed in their Sunday best, carrying purses, guiding two little children inside for the morning service.

"I guess a murder can happen anywhere. In hindsight, ladies, it's probably a good thing we didn't have a gun back in Jordan or I might not have lived to tell this tale."

Hannah reaches over to give Callie a hug. "Goodness gracious, to think we might never have known this dear, sweet daughter of yours."

Nellie stands and stretches, then yawns while placing her hands against the small of her back. "I'm getting awfully stiff, Will. I think we should go back to the house, finish up over refreshments."

"Oh, hush, Nellie," says Hannah. "You heard what Will said. He'll not be telling Uncle Amer's story over teacups and lace doilies. Wouldn't be fitting. Now sit down. I want to hear the rest."

"Well, I declare!" spouts Nellie.

I grin and wink at Hannah who smiles back.

"Declare all you want, Nell. Move around a bit if you like, but we're not leaving this cemetery until I get to the end of my story." I glance over at the corner plot where Amer's tombstone should be. "It's the least we can do for him."

We all stand and stretch. After a few jumping jacks, Cal saunters over to the big cottonwood tree. I half expect her to start climbing its lower branch. If ever there's a tree to scale, she'll often give it a go—even at her age.

My cousins straighten out their handkerchiefs on the bench's wooden slats and lower themselves once again, as if aiming for a target. Cal plops down on the grass with her shoulders against the massive tree trunk. Pieces of last summer's cottonwood fluff float through the air. A robin sings while the sun heads far into the west.

I sit down with a freshly lit pipe. One more bowl of sweet tobacco should be enough to see us through to the end.

"Now where was I?"

"On your way to the undertaking parlor," says Cal, glancing up at my cousins.

"Though I don't think any of us would really want to go there," says Nell.

"Yah, yah." Hannah takes a deep breath, as if ready to blow out a cluster of candles. "It seems we've been avoiding the inevitable," she says.

I clench and draw on the stem of my pipe while stacking the last of Amer's letters on the bench next to me. "Yes, well, it wasn't easy."

After that unnerving encounter with the Carmichaels and the gunshot on Main Street, my heart was still in my throat as we approached the stoop of yet another white frame building; this one reflected greater investment and outward upkeep than the others—fresh paint, a clean picket fence, flowers around the foundation; a lucrative undertaking, that sort of business.

I jumped a foot when I heard, then saw, who was behind the door. Before Dad could knock, the hinges creaked and an eerie voice said, "I've been watching for you. Come in, please. For a moment, I thought more customers would be stretchered in, delivered to my cellar."

We didn't laugh and neither did he. Dad and I soon found out Mr. Hawkins wasn't the joking kind.

It was as dim inside that entry as a darkened nickelodeon, where your eyes are slow to adjust and you can hear the racing notes of a violin or a piano playing along with Buster Keaton's antics. But here, there were no gaudy posters or the sounds of a piano or a violin. And no comedy. Instead, the undertaker materialized from behind the door. His looks matched his voice.

Henry Hawkins was tall and thin, angular, dressed in black—a suit too tight, even for a skinny man. He had a long, narrow face and a high forehead. He wasn't exactly bald, but it was a long stretch before you saw his hairline. He fixed us with strange, pool-like eyes, as if he had gazed too long at grisly work. His smile, when it relaxed, twisted into an odd grimace. Tilting his head, he bowed slightly. Then holding out a limp hand, as if using a cane, he turned and glided over to a small table with a lamp on it. He seemed a touch too practiced, as if he were following his undertaker's manual to a T. Here was a keeper of the dead, a man who gave me the willies.

Mr. Hawkins struck a match and lit the wick of his hurricane lamp. After adjusting the flame, slowly replacing its chimney, then readjusting the glow, he took up the lamp and motioned for us to follow him as he oiled his way from the darkened parlor, along a narrow corridor, through a tiny door (we had to duck to avoid hitting our heads on a rafter), and down rough-hewn steps. Despite the warm, dry weather, the basement was dim and dank. Our sunshiny day was over for the time being, forgotten once we'd gone down into that musty cellar.

The lamp threw ghostly shadows against clay walls and over a hard-packed dirt floor. Except for the peculiar odors, that place reminded me of our root cellar back home. But instead of giving off the smells of stored carrots and squash and apples, this bone-chilling room smelled of saltpeter, like an ancient cemetery on a rainy night when the faint odor of decaying corpses rises up through the ground.

At first, I was appalled to find my uncle in such a place: a dirt basement. But then, I thought, why not? Amer had been a farmer all his life. Nearly everything of importance to him was of the earth: his soddy; those dusty trails; the land he worked; even the burial plot waiting for him in Rockford. So it all made sense. Why not an earthen mortuary? As Amer would likely have said, "It is clean dirt."

My eyes soon adjusted to the gloom and to the rows of cosmetics and pastes lined up on a narrow table next to one wall. Against another wall stood a tall desk with a three-by-three-foot Coroner's Book. Strange paraphernalia hung from large hooks pounded into the clay—most likely embalming tubes and such. The smell of formaldehyde made me nauseous, a little woozy. I expected Dad would feel the same way, but he stood tall and straight, wearing an expression that hadn't changed since breakfast. Or, for that matter, since we'd received the terrible news four days earlier, back on our farm outside of Hadley.

I'd felt lonely, and somewhat irritated, that my father had so little to say during our train trip and the journey from Forsyth to Jordan with Mr. Malloy at the wheel of that motorized stage. But by the time we left the hotel that morning, I recalled what Dad had told me the night before: "No matter what the situation, Will, do what you have to do in a dignified way." There in the mortuary basement, I realized he was trying to stay calm and steady for my sake. I looked to him and held onto his strength more than ever, inside that nightmarish cellar.

Mr. Hawkins carried his oil lamp toward the center of the room and hung it from a hook in the beamed ceiling, directly above a jerry-rigged table with a cloth draped over it. Beneath the white cloth lay my uncle's lifeless form.

By age sixteen, I'd shot plenty of game and held dead and dying animals. But, as I said before, I'd never seen a dead person. Standing next to that bulging, draped cloth, I was awestruck, yet inquisitive, wanting to see him, but not like that.

Maybe there was some mistake, I told myself, and this wasn't Uncle Amer. Wouldn't it be wonderful, I thought, if this were a mix-up, and he had simply left to go fishing at Fort Peck Lake without telling anyone? Just as I'd imagined on the train, this could be a case of mistaken identity. Although unusual and far-fetched, things like that do happen. Don't they?

With both hands, Mr. Hawkins slowly reached over to pinch the top corners of that sheet between thumbs and index fingers. With a flourish, as if unveiling a work of art, he peeled back the cover. My legs began to grow weak and started to tremble. I felt a hard throbbing in my head as my heart began to beat faster and faster. Blood surged through my veins like a whitewater river.

Naked, except for a cloth draped across his privates, Uncle Amer's straight-limbed body lay there on the table, thin—skeletal thin—making him appear taller than he actually was. His torso was the color of flax, which made his face, lower neck, forearms and hands look all the more sunburnt, like shades of copper. His hair was swept back, revealing a white forehead. I was shocked by the peaceful look on his face—as if he hadn't known any violence. He appeared as innocent as a youngster, vulnerable and alone, lonely even, yet wanting privacy. I felt as though we had intruded.

Mr. Hawkins urged us to step closer, in order to see the bullet holes. Both Dad and I bristled at the sight of them.

The undertaker matter-of-factly pointed out and explained each one: "Your brother, Mr. Lindstrom, was shot twice with a .45 caliber. He took the first in the abdomen. The fatal bullet grazed his right arm and went in three inches below the nipple on the left side, over the seventh rib, then ranged downward, coming out toward the back of the eleventh rib. It penetrated the lung and passed just below the heart."

The wounds were clean, but the holes were large and the skin around them had turned black. Mr. Hawkins said that as he was undressing Amer, one of the flattened bullets tumbled from his clothes. He took it over to Sheriff Fleming.

"The bullets hadn't hit any vital organs, except for the one lung," said the mortician. "That's why your brother didn't die right away. He would have experienced much pain on breathing. It's possible he could have been saved, if he'd received immediate help. If we'd had the means. I'm sorry to say he simply bled out."

'Could have been saved, if . . .' is not something you like to hear. What good did that comment do us? Dad slowly shook his head and moved in closer.

As long as I live, I'll never forget what happened next. Just as Mr. Hawkins began telling us he would ready the rough box and corpse for the long journey back to Rockford, Dad leaned over the slab and gathered Amer up and into his arms. Making little choking sounds, he held his brother tight against his chest for a long time before easing him back onto the table. Tenderly, he touched the skin around each of the bullet holes, then drew the sheet up around Amer's shoulders and neck as if he were tucking him in for the night. With his rough brown fingers, he touched Amer's paper-white forehead, and then lightly swept them across his hair.

When Dad finally turned to look at me, his eyes glistened, and his expression had changed. For the first time in three days, he had taken on that clenched look I saw on the faces of those ranchers back at the hotel. His eyes brimmed and turned from pale blue to nearly white.

I fought the urge to cry. When my legs began to buckle, Dad reached an arm around my waist to steady and bolster me up until I could hold my ground. I can feel it to this day—my father's strength. It coursed through me like the unwavering current from a trickle charger.

"This is just the shell of him, Willie," he whispered. "Always remember that. It's only the shell."

I have never forgotten what my father taught me that day: When someone dies, the casing is all that's left. What is essential rises up out of that shell to become a part of the whole.

"As long as we remember," he said, trying to keep his lips from quivering, "the dead are never truly dead."

I had more growing up to do before those words could really take hold, giving me a rock-steady sense that the dead will always stay with us in their own way, as if they've simply slipped off into the next room, some place nearby, just around the corner.

Yes, I had more seasons to work through.

As we turned to go back up the narrow steps, I glanced one last time at Uncle Amer lying there on that slab, and imagined him saying, "I did my best to make a go of it."

In spite of what Dad had just told me, I felt as though we were abandoning him. I did not want to turn my back on my uncle. And it troubled me to think that Mother and Ray would never have the chance to say their goodbyes, not even at the funeral in Rockford.

Although the sunshine hurt my eyes for a moment, I was glad to see that light of day after climbing up and out of the cellar. Mr. Hawkins said little else, just that he'd have a pine box set to go whenever we were ready to leave Jordan. Quickly and efficiently, he showed us out of his white-framed house the same way we'd come in.

I began to breathe easier when I saw Mr. Malloy lingering, once again, in front of the hotel. This time, he was standing with several towns-people who had gathered around to admire his stage. While our driver showed them the engine, explaining and demonstrating how it worked, Dad and I collected our luggage from inside the hotel, and paid for the night's lodging, including Mr. Malloy's. The desk clerk, appearing stiff and stern, said nothing about the Carmichaels' arrest or the sheriff's warning shot or how it must have affected us. He simply thanked my father in the same clipped manner as the night before.

THE DRIVE OUT to Amer's land took about half an hour through dust and dry land vegetation: sagebrush, buckwheat, western wheatgrass. Mr. Malloy pointed out a yellow-flowered plant called curlycup gum-weed, which the Indians used for medicinal purposes. "The bees like it too," he said. "Makes good honey."

A batch of greasewood shrubs, found in alkaline soil, reminded me of where that old geezer lived, off the trail between Forsyth and Jordan—the guy with the gun and the whiskey bottle.

I asked how any crops could grow without irrigation during such a dry spell.

"They don't," said Mr. Malloy. "After the rains stopped and the drought began, nothing could thrive. Take a look at farmers' faces; that'll tell you most everything after conditions became severe out here, then grew worse."

When he said that, I remembered those faces at breakfast time, back at the hotel—how you could read it in their eyes and in the set of their mouths. To this day, I can still picture them, some sitting back with their arms folded tight across their chests, others balancing their work-worn hands at the edge of the table.

Amer's `dobe and timbered corral rose up in the distance like a tiny fort. As we drew closer, it became obvious that the place was abandoned. With the horses gone, there was no sign of life, not even a bird. And no Radge to herd any of 'em. Where was that frisky dog Amer had written about?

The air was filled with the smells of a hot sun cooking the earth and bent-over cornstalks. At several spots next to his fields, Amer had piled mounds of stones cleared from his land in order to work the soil and plant crops. Those heaps of boulders reminded me of ancient burial sites.

His soddy

I hesitated for some minutes before entering the sod house; here was everything of importance to my uncle: his past; his hopes for the future; the door to his world, inside and out. It didn't feel right to walk in without Amer there to greet us, to show us around, eager and proud of all the hard work he had done, and how he and his horses had plowed and seeded together with Radge alongside. I turned to look at the acres of corn they'd planted, but the soil and the crops were parched, dwarfed, barely recognizable—so unlike our fields at home: tall, green, uniform rows.

"Just sit back now, boys, and watch 'em grow," Amer used to say, clicking his beer bottle against our soda pops. It was obvious that such a thing wasn't going to happen then, near Jordan.

Still, I could see what he loved about this place: day and night that enormous sky and broad horizon, as wide as it is deep, soared over the land version of a great ocean; the packed glitter of stars shone down, alternating with sunrise and sunset on the acreage he worked. How small is a man under all of that? Convinced of its possibilities, Amer had been willing to drive himself until he broke. And yet, for starters, here was his planting, albeit wilted and thirsting for rain. And here was the solid earthen home he had built for himself with the aid of a turf cutter tool, a wheelbarrow, and help from John and Mary McKamman.

"Like they do in Ireland," explained Mr. Malloy. "You have to clear the upper layers of stems and tough roots before you can cut your bricks." He demonstrated the motions with an imaginary turf spade. "Make your cut on two sides, like this. Then with a single twist you've got a brick."

He held out his hands to show the dimensions of a sizeable slab of sod, then dusted his palms as if he'd just stacked a row. "The top layers we use for fuel."

On a rickety crate near the entry of my uncle's soddy sat a large clay pot filled with dried soil tamped around withered brown stems, brittle leaves and faded flowers. In the center of that dying plant, one red blossom spoke geranium.

After gazing at the single flower, I stepped inside the 'dobe and was immediately struck by how comfortable Amer had made it. His sod bricks were evenly stacked. Soaked newspaper, rags, and mud filled the cracks. A hard-packed floor didn't even resemble dirt; sprinkled with water and apparently swept often, it was free of dust, hard as cement. Amer had plastered the walls with a mixture of clay and ashes for a whitewash effect, and reinforced the ceiling with timbers and tarpaper in order to support the sod roof. A few stringy roots dangled from above the rafters, but because of the drought, no rainwater had as yet seeped through the inevitable cracks and holes. No puddles. No streaks of mud. It was a fine shelter, dry, well-chinked, homey, ready for winter.

Because he lived alone, Amer had no reason to partition his space with blankets for privacy. It remained one large room, neat and clean. His narrow bed was made up with a brightly colored quilt, likely stitched together by Mary McKamman. A single wooden chair, one solid crate, and a small table, covered with a clean square of blue-flowered oilcloth, stood against a wall to the right of entry. The oilcloth reminded me of what Mother used on our table back home, spread the length of a long set of boards once strewn with maps and railroad brochures in a kitchen alive with chatter and excitement over Amer's plans and upcoming trip.

Beneath his table lay a medium trap door with an iron ring. I shoved the little table aside, raised the door, and looked down into a dark hole. The air was cool inside a recess big enough for a large crock of milk, which Dad and I lifted up onto the table along with several pounds of butter, a bag of potatoes, and jars of butchered meat sealed in brine.

"We'll see that the McKammans get this food," he said.

I placed the cover back over the now empty hole and turned to explore the rest of the room.

There, on a homemade shelf, were Amer's books with faded blue and green and gray spines aligned as perfectly as a row of corn: Shakespeare, Cervantes, Longfellow, Cooper, Willa Cather, Jonathan Swift, Charles Dickens. I imagined Uncle Amer reading and re-reading these volumes, especially in winter, when there would be little else to do, except looking after the animals and waiting for spring to break through. Warm and cozy. I wondered, though, about the fifty-gallon drum filled with kerosene—so old it was the color of Mars.

"OH, NO, SAYS NELLIE, abruptly. "He used kerosene inside that soddy?"

Hannah shakes her head. "Bad stuff. Our uncle Benoni had one of those drums inside his little bachelor shack in Davis Junction. That's how he kept warm in winter."

106

"Burning kerosene in closed quarters?" asks Cal. "Isn't that really dangerous?"

"I should say so!" says Hannah. "It was cheap heat and not uncommon years ago. But over time the fumes made people sick. Uncle Benoni, for example. He was always feeling poorly."

"He smelled funny, too," says Nell. "Strange. His clothes and skin. I'm sure it was the kerosene seeping from his pores. He was always so thin and pale. We couldn't help but feel sorry for the poor man."

"Didn't you encourage him to stop using it?" asks Cal. "It would have been safer to burn wood."

"Oh, no. He was an old bachelor. We would never have thought to tell him how to live his life. Women just don't do that, you know."

Cal and I exchange glances, knowing precisely what it is about Nell's remark that doesn't fly with us.

Chapter 11

His Master's Face

WITH MR. MALLOY'S HELP, Dad and I faced the grim task of packing up Uncle Amer's belongings: family pictures, several dozen books (including the novel by Oscar Wilde, whose beige cover had become soiled and frayed), a few clothes, his shaving mug and brush—the same things he had packed when he left our farm in Hadley. As for the implements and tools he'd purchased in Forsyth and Jordan, those would go to the McKammans.

We packed his phonograph and the dark red album storage book embossed with Victor Records and its trademark painting of Nipper. With his head cocked before the horn, that white Terrier with black ears focused intently into an Edison Bell cylinder, touched by the recording of his dead master's voice.

Inside the album, well-worn sleeves contained Amer's prized celluloids, including Enrico Caruso singing *Tosca*, and Florence Easton's character, Lauretta, singing *O Mio Babbino Caro*.

"Just because that aria belongs to a woman," Amer once said, "I see no reason why a man can't sing it too, if he feels like it—especially out in his fields with no one there to call him on it."

The violin that had accompanied his singing was the last item to leave the soddy, its smooth, scuffed wood coated with a thin layer of dust, and its frets a tad grimy with seasons of in-grained dirt. Dad carefully wrapped the instrument in Amer's blue chambray work shirt. Just as he was nesting it on top of the luggage at the rear of the stage, the McKammans arrived, having walked the distance from their homestead.

John's sunburned, freckled face shone with good health. His pale red hair held a neat part on the right side. He wore fresh work clothes. Except for one thing, John resembled the ranchers and farmers who had ridden into town for breakfast that morning. The noticeable difference—merry eyes, twinkling and cheery.

And so were the eyes of Mary McKamman. She stood tall and sturdy, a bit hefty, with grayish brown hair pulled back tightly in a bun. Her broad smile revealed deep dimples. She immediately reached out to give me a strong, motherly hug, then kept an arm around my shoulders for an extra moment. I could see why Uncle Amer liked her. She and John were every bit as good-hearted as he had described them in his letters—the kind of people you want to be around because, like the best of family members, they give you the feeling that anything is possible, that you are cared for, and that any hardship can be overcome. Hope and an indomitable spirit—that's what the McKammans were made of. And they set out to lift ours that day.

"It's powerful sorry we are," said John, shaking Dad's hand and then my own, as well as Mr. Malloy's.

"We're missing him every day," said Mary. "Early of a morning, I look for Amer out workin' a section with those four horses and Radge trotting alongside. Stayed close by, he did, that fetching dog of his."

I asked where Radge was. John said they had taken him in, along with the horses, but had to tether him to a stake because he kept running back here to look for Amer.

"Can't you hear him?" he asked, cupping an ear.

I listened and caught the sound of a mid-sized dog barking from a short distance away.

"A smart one, he is. About this high." John lowered his hand toward the ground. "A fine Border Collie, black and white."

"Suren, that Radge is a fine dog," said Mrs. McKamman. "But he misses his master. Runs off in search of him whenever he gets the chance. Out in the fields, wandering along a trail, among the rocks and stones. That's where we find Radge.

"Well, then, when you've finished here, John and I would have you come by our place to see him and the horses. And for coffee and eats."

Dad made sure that the last of Amer's possessions were securely piled on the rear seat of the stage, while I walked over to close the 'dobe door, all the while wondering what would become of this little house. Would it fall to ruin or would some other honyocker eventually move in? Another farmer as committed as Amer was to carve out a place for himself.

Whoever entered this soddy wouldn't find it completely empty. There would be that old kerosene stove the color of Mars, and the makeshift bookshelf, along with a third item: during one last look around, I had noticed a gleam coming from one corner of the shelf—gold lettering on the spine of a single volume propped in the shadows, its brownish-green color blending in with the wood. The front cover was embossed with vines and leaves and golden roots trailing from the title—*Leaves of Grass*. I opened it to the 1891 copyright page, and then read a little of the first poem, "Song of Myself." The third line stood out: "For every atom belonging to me as good belongs to you."

I might have taken that book of poems, but everything else had been packed and tied down inside the stage. Besides, something about *Leaves of Grass* just made it seem right to let it be, let it stay there in the midst of that field. So I left it for whoever might occupy Amer's shelter in months to come. Or years. And if the soddy collapsed, well then...

Mr. Malloy started up his Cadillac. Dad helped John and Mary get into the middle seat. Then he and I took our usual places next to the driver. But Mr. Malloy didn't leave right away. He sat there for a moment with his hands atop the wheel, letting the car idle as he glanced around. Before we could ask if there was a problem or if we'd forgotten something, he stepped out of his car and walked over to the well, took down the big ladle hanging from a hook, and turned to dip water from the shallow bit left on the bottom of the horse trough—as if he were going to drink it. Instead, he hurried back to pour the water onto that dying geranium standing near the soddy door.

Dad brought his hand to his mouth. No one spoke. For me, at age sixteen, a feeling ran through my mind that I'd never experienced before. And later on in life, I would learn what the word 'metaphor' meant, and how it connected to what Mr. Malloy had done.

He returned the pewter dipper to its hook, got back in the car, and drove that half-mile to the McKammans' soddy. The rest of us, in silence, held on our laps many of the things that would soon belong to John and Mary: Amer's kitchen supplies, food from the storage hole beneath his trap door, a few books, a pair of pants and a shirt, small implements collected during those months of hard work.

All the rest we would take home with us, back to Hadley, including the shotgun. Never did find his revolver.

Amer's horses, corralled next to the road in front of the McKammans' place, were nicely filled out—muscular, with coats shining in the sun. When I asked Mr. McKamman about their names and which was which, he stroked their faces, one at a time, pointing at Sam, then Johnny, Skeeky, and Rounder, who began bobbing his head up and down as though he were greeting me.

I started to laugh, remembering what Amer had written about taking a nosedive while working his field late one afternoon. As he'd leaned over to dig up a large stone, Rounder lowered his head, nudged his master from behind, and pushed him down. Curling his lips, he whinnied softly. Amer stood up, showed his own teeth, and started to dance in front of the horses, along with a barking Radge. Just as a rain shower moved in, he hollered, "It's a good day for ducks, Rounder! Not horses! Just ducks!"

Amer also wrote about how those horses smelled in the rain, as well as during a good brushing after long hours in the fields. He'd treated them well and it showed. In return, he said, they'd given him their best:

long hard work, friendly little nudges, soft whinnies, and nicker sounds whenever he sang and danced around them.

That quartet now stood still, focusing on us with bright eyes, nodding heads, and tails swishing. Even their ears pricked forward as we greeted them. If they could talk, what would they say? "Where's Amer?" What could they tell us? "Whenever it rains," they might murmur, "it's a good day for ducks."

Radge, alert to our arrival, leapt up and down, barking in excitement, shaking the dust from his coat. I was so excited to see that smiling snout Amer had so accurately described in his letters—a happy grin as the dog cut and ran and chased those night birds across the fields. As soon as I approached, he stopped jumping and strained at his tether, whining, desperate for attention.

While the McKammans stood nearby, Dad leaned over to greet Radge, placing his hands on either side of the dog's face, as one would a child who then glances back with loving eyes and a warm smile.

As soon as I moved in, he hunkered low and wagged his tail, inviting me to play. Right then and there, I wanted to take that pup home with us. I could tell my brother the dog was meant for him. Then maybe Ray wouldn't feel so bad about having to stay back on the farm with Mother, after I had been the one chosen to accompany our dad.

I played with Radge for several minutes, hopping back and forth, laughing and talking to him, and then sat down on the ground so he could rest his muzzle on my knee. With one stroke along his thick coat, it became obvious that he was still sore where his ribs had been broken by Tom Carmichael's boot. He looked up at me with such eyes—a longing, somewhat desperate look—and whimpered when I tethered him again and headed for the soddy door. I wouldn't have left the dog, only I didn't want to miss out on what the McKammans had to say about my uncle's last hours.

Because the two bullets fired from Tom Carmichael's .45 caliber revolver hadn't hit any vital organs, other than one lung, Amer lived long enough to tell his side of the story. If only he could have made it to a hospital; but there wasn't any close by. Besides, with such slow and bumpy transportation, he likely wouldn't have made it. Smooth and speedy was non-existent in those days. So, as undertaker Hawkins had explained, Amer just laid there and bled out—bled out while describing the details of his own murder.

AT SUNRISE THAT MORNING, Amer and John McKamman went out to their respective fields; John McKamman planting corn; Amer with his four horses hitched to a disk drill, working the oblong field near a division marker.

Instead of settling into his own labor, Tom Carmichael stomped into view, pacing up and down the fence line along the adjacent land, acting testy, lashing out at his team of horses that patiently stood nearby.

"Screaming at the air like one possessed," is how John described him.

Amer made an effort to ignore that scene by keeping at his work. Around noon, he tried to get through the common gate, but couldn't without great difficulty. Carmichael had deliberately wired it shut with doubled hogwire, staples, and a web halter strap to delay Amer's getting out when he broke for dinner.

When Tom rode up on horseback with his .45 drawn and cocked, Amer ran back to one of his draft horses for the rifle he'd strapped to his side. But before he could get at the saddle holster, Tom fired that first shot, which grazed Amer's arm and lodged in his stomach. He doubled over and took cover behind the horses who got too excited and milled out of control. Tom squeezed off a second bullet—the one that entered Amer's chest—then turned sharply and galloped away, likely assuming that he had shot him dead.

His rifle hanging askew in the saddle holster, Amer lay bleeding there on the ground, while his horses lowered their heads to check on him.

"Suren, if only he'd had his revolver," said John. "Why he left it behind, Mary and I will always wonder. You see, it was more than once those Carmichaels taunted and threatened him fierce. Shoved him off the footpath in town. Knocked him down. Then came that awful beating."

Dad didn't say anything to the McKammans about not finding the gun. Someone must have gone into the soddy and taken it, because I never saw it either.

"That Carmichael," said Mary, shaking her head. "The look of a man I never liked." She curled the edge of her apron as if rolling a bandage. "Oh, the face on him. Those eyes. Hungry for the land and no heart. The way he drives his sheep, whippin' 'em as if they was mules. Beyond the pale, it is. Beyond the pale."

"I know Amer was a crack shot," said John. "A fine trap shooter back in Minnesota. Like you, Vic. Suren, he could have picked Carmichael off at long range."

"Och, aye, 'tis a shame." Mary slowly shook her head. "But he didn't have it in him to kill."

"True it is." John poured a little of his coffee from cup to saucer, then sipped the cooled liquid, holding the saucer between his thumb and two fingers. "Radge barked like fury," he said, setting the saucer back on the square wooden table. "Then the gunshots. We ran down the road and saw Amer stooped over, hugging his chest and stomach. He staggered and dropped, then picked himself up and made a few more paces before falling down again. By the time we reached him, he was crawling along the fence line with Radge tight by his side. He took off his work gloves—full of dust and blood they were—and passed them to Mary. Calm-like, he asked us to take him to town—to the doctor."

With pinched lips and a trembling chin, John gazed at his wife for a moment before continuing. "Another neighbor came a-running. Fought in the Great War, he had. Tended plenty of the injured. Mr. Armstrong took one look at Amer's wounds and told him he wouldn't live long enough to make it to Jordan. Sometimes it hurts to be honest. But honest is how he had to be.

John turned to point at a shelf against one wall of their soddy. "Mary keeps a store of medicines and bandages here at home, so we loaded your uncle into Armstrong's Chevrolet and drove the half-mile back home with Radge running alongside. Armstrong was right. Amer couldn't have stood the longer, bumpy ride into town. His only chance would be to get the doctor out here to our place in time to remove the bullets and patch him up before he lost too much blood.

"Mr. Armstrong, Mary, and I got Amer out of the car, carried him inside, and placed him on that cot over there. He wasn't very heavy." John stared for a moment at that part of the room. "Mary stayed by him while Armstrong and I drove apace into town for the sheriff and the doctor. We decided to go together, our revolvers at the ready, in case Tom Carmichael and his brothers were lurking nearby."

"And Radge stayed next to him too," said Mary. "That dog never left his side, kept vigil every second until the very end. Och, the terrible pain Amer endured. He tried to bear up, your one. Aye, he fixed his hands on his chest, just so. But suren, it got the better of him."

To this day, I can hear Mary's sweet voice, her Irish brogue. And I can see her otherwise cheerful eyes tear up as she told us about Amer's last moments:

"I did what I could to comfort him," she said softly. "Gentle he was, our dear, dear friend. Never wishin' to sow harm upon a soul. 'Suren, Mr. Lindstrom,' I says, 'you'll be pullin' through this. You've got work a-plenty to do on your place.'

"He spoke witness." Mary McKamman reached for her worn, black leather Bible and opened it to the page where she had recorded his testimony. "It's all here, it is. He even put down his name."

I could have wept when she read us his words: "I, Amer Lindstrom, expecting to die, do make this statement, true, so help me God."

"After the signing," said Mary, "Amer whispered something I'll remember all my days, I will. He said, 'I guess Tom Carmichael didn't care for my music.'"

Where had I heard that before? In one of his letters to us.

"Would Amer had his revolver," said John, "he might have stood a chance. But you know, Mr. Lindstrom, my Mary is right. Your brother just didn't have it in him to fight."

"He struggled and poured sweat would he be working a field at midday," said Mary. "Every breath he took made him double up. Cry out in pain. Radge cried too, and turned in tight circles. I did my best to soothe Amer. Washed the dirt and dust from his face and hands. Stroked his arms—those he still held tight to his chest. He bled through all the bandages, so I used feed sack towels to pack the wounds and staunch the bleeding.

"After a time, he settled down and stared up into my face like he was searching for something. His eyes—soft, they were. And wide open. Such beautiful clear blue eyes." Mary shook her head slowly. "I'll never forget our dear Swede, Amer Lindstrom. Lovely, he was. I gave him back my tenderest smile. You see, I thought he might be remembering his mother and, would I do that, why, it would help ease him out and into heaven. He used to talk about his mother, you know—Ernestine. Said she died young. Left a good number of children, she did."

Mary McKamman stopped talking in order to collect herself. John reached over to pat her hand. After dabbing at her eyes with a corner of her apron, she continued. "As I said, Radge stood by Amer the whole time, nudging him with his nose, whining softly until the end—and for a long time after. Amer tried so hard to stay, but it was no good. He looked like a boy, really, a tired boy just in from the fields, ready for a good rest. He gazed down at his dog for a time, dropped his arm onto Radge's shoulder, and drifted off to sleep. After a bit, he stopped breathing."

As Mary whispered those last words to the rest of us gathered around her table, the sun edged toward the horizon. Dust motes traveled slowly along a shaft of light burning in through a rippled windowpane.

She explained how she had gently closed my uncle's eyes with her fingertips, and placed coins on his eyelids. When she drew the blanket up over Amer's face, Radge cried and pawed at the cover. Mary quickly lowered that blanket and comforted the dog until he settled down.

"You must understand," she said, "that dog wasn't ready for his master's face to be hidden from sight."

The two of them kept vigil—Mary in her straight-back chair, Radge standing next to the cot with his muzzle resting on Amer's arm.

"We waited like that," she said, "until John and Mr. Armstrong returned with the sheriff and the doctor."

For a long moment, the five of us sat silent, listening to Amer's dog barking outside, nonstop. A sudden wind whistled through the cracks between the window frames and sod walls. The lowering sun caught a few of the dust motes still circling in the changing light.

John spoke in low tones. "He's caught rotten now, is Tom Carmichael."

Dad nodded once and lifted his cup for a final swallow of the strong coffee. He stood and thanked Mary and John for their kindness, said he'd never forget all they had done for his brother, and reminded them to keep the animals, the timbers from their corral, and Amer's farm equipment and tools.

"Mind yourselves now," said John, facing my dad. "Safe journey."

Taking leave of the McKammans was as difficult as any goodbye I've ever experienced. Not only were they good and caring people, offering warm hugs and tears, they were our final link to the last days of Uncle Amer. And I knew we'd never see them again.

Chapter 12

A Song That Would Like to Make You Cry

BACK IN JORDAN, Dad bought a length of rope and rented a small two-wheeled trailer for hauling the rough box that had been placed upstairs in the undertaker's parlor. Someone must have helped Mr. Hawkins carry my uncle up from that chilly cellar. He was dressed and laid out with yards and yards of soft packing cloth to keep him from rolling hard against the sides of the pine coffin during our bumpy ride back to the train station.

Seeing that we were satisfied with how he had prepared the body, Mr. Hawkins laid down a shroud from head to toe, added more packing cloth, and brought forth a hammer to nail the lid shut. For good measure, he cinched two long straps around each end of the box.

While he and Dad took care of financial matters, I helped Mr. Malloy lash the temporary coffin onto the trailer hitched to the stage. Then we left Jordan and retraced the distance back to Forsyth, with Radge sitting next to me. That Border Collie stayed tight by my side for the next ten years—one of the most loving dogs we ever had.

The other passengers were a man and his wife, expecting a baby any day. Although Jordan had a doctor, the woman insisted on traveling to the hospital in Forsyth, a town where they had relatives. I remember noticing her condition, then looking back at the rough box bouncing along behind the stage on that long, dusty trail—one gone, another on the way.

After dropping the expectant couple off at the hospital, Mr. Malloy delivered Dad, Radge, and me to the depot just in time to book the next train bound for Miles City. From there, we would travel to Chicago, then on to Rockford.

The three of us unloaded the pine coffin and placed it in a small holding room cooled by blocks of ice. Radge laid down on the floor next to the coffin and refused to budge. He looked up at me with eyes that seemed more human than those of an animal. I stayed by his side for a time, alternately patting the pine box and petting him.

Radge kept gazing up at the coffin and so did I, remembering how Amer had been tucked in, and what he had looked like lying on the table in Mr. Hawkin's mortuary cellar. And then I recalled how lovingly Mrs. McKamman had treated my uncle. I was convinced that her presence and goodness-filled eyes, along with those of Radge, had seeped into the ebb and flow of Amer's brain, so that the last images he could perceive, and hold onto, would cancel out that fiendish face of the man who had drawn his gun.

Finally, I rigged up a leash for our dog from a length of rope that had been tied to the trailer. Radge and I joined the others on the train platform, where he took a long drink of water from one of Mr. Malloy's canteens, and ate a large slice of bread also handed to him. When our driver offered up a chunk of apple, Radge swept the platform with his tail, barked twice, as if to say "ap-ple," pawed at the air, and tossed his head in ecstacy.

Dad settled with Mr. Malloy, who agreed to return the trailer to Jordan on his next trip back. We shook hands several times, sorry to part company. He told us he felt as bad for Amer as if he were his own brother. Dad offered him five more dollars. At first, Mr. Malloy refused it, but Dad said, "No, that's your'n. You've a right to it."

Although a dollar was hard to come by back in those days, I was pleased, and proud of my Dad for doing that.

We heard the "All aboard" and had to rush to make sure the coffin got transferred from the holding room to the train's baggage compartment (Radge would ride there too). We shook hands again and clapped one another on the shoulders, as reluctant in our leave-taking with Mr. Malloy as we were with the McKammans. Even then, he didn't turn his back on us until long after the train had left the station. I watched and waved from the window. We were almost out of sight when I saw him return to his car.

For two days and nights we rode along on the rails, clickety-clack, clickety-clack, and when we reached Chicago, discovered there was no branch train scheduled for Rockford until the next day. We had to leave the coffin in another ice-cooled holding room at the depot and take a taxi to the Palmer House Hotel. I tied Radge to a stake in the yard behind the kitchen and set out a big bowl of water and table scraps gathered up by the cook who had a dog of his own. After a light supper, Dad and I fell into bed.

"SO THERE YOU HAVE IT, LADIES. When I asked my dad about the funeral plans and about Amer's burial, he said that your folks, Uncle Frank and Uncle Ed, were in charge of the arrangements." I point the stem of my pipe toward the plots across the way. "He was to go in next to Grandma Ernestine and Auntie Edna."

"My, oh, my," says Nellie. "That was some trip for you and Vic."

"Unforgettable is all I can say."

"That's right," says Callie. "I grew up hearing Dad's story ever since I was a little girl. Some day, I might write it up for him."

I smiled and nodded at my daughter. "Early the next morning, we made sure the pine box was intact and carefully brought aboard the Illinois Central for the last leg of our journey here to Rockford."

"It's certainly too bad your mother and brother couldn't have come for the funeral," says Hannah.

"That's for sure! I wished the same thing. It might have made a difference in how Ray and I got along after that. Oh, much later we had some fun years together, especially when we were in our twenties, driving to all those big dance halls filled with swing music and pretty girls: Valhalla, Hollyhock, the Arkota. But then he married Eloise and everything went to hell in a hand basket. Now, I think he's in a nursing home. Not entirely sure, but that's where he's likely ended up."

In order to clean my pipe, I reach inside my suit jacket for the gold penknife hanging from a delicate golden chain connected to the pocket watch I received from Mother and Dad on my twenty-first birthday. Ray got one too.

"It's too bad my brother can't be here with us now—at least for the aftermath. You know, I've always wished that he could have been in on all of this, even my telling of Amer's story from beginning to end."

Cal gets up from her spot next to the cottonwood tree. "Wasn't there some way for him and Gram to be here for the funeral?" she asks, brushing off her slacks.

"Nope. It was too big a trip in those days. And costly. Besides, they couldn't leave the livestock. We had a good-sized dairy herd. Pigs and chickens. A couple of dogs, a bunch of cats. Dad told Ray that he was counting on him to take care of everything on our farm. So they had to stay put."

"Yah, yah," says Hannah. "You can't let the animals go even for a day, especially those milk cows."

Using the penknife hooked to my watch chain, I loosen the charred pipe tobacco, and tap the bowl against the heel of my shoe; dark flecks sprinkle onto the ground. Overhead, the pine boughs and cottonwood leaves hang completely still. Sunshine angles low across the cemetery, reflecting off the field of headstones. It's not so warm as when we first arrived. And the distant droning sound of highway traffic has picked up.

"After all these years," I say, glancing at my cousins, "just imagine. Ten days from the day he died until the funeral, and Uncle Amer's remains could be shown in all likeness of himself. That undertaker in Jordan may have been strange, kind of creepy even, but he knew his trade. Yes siree, Mr. Hawkins did right by Amer."

"May our uncle rest in peace," says Hannah, waving a hand toward the supposèd plot.

She and Nellie rise slowly from their bench and, with stiff moves, snatch up the handkerchiefs they were sitting on, tuck them into their purses, then shuffle about, a little wobbly, until they can find a balance. Their pastel skirts flutter in a sudden puff of wind.

Cal steps over to the bench, gathers Amer's letters for me and reties the bundle with the same soft piece of creamy cotton string that has held them together for seventy years.

"I'm glad we came to Rockford, Dad. And I'm happy that you could tell us all about Amer right here in this cemetery." She grins and cocks her head. "No teacups. No lace doilies."

"I was finally able to get to the end of it, Cal. But it's a hell of a thing to find no marker—such a disappointment. And nothing more for Grandma and Auntie."

She hands me the packet of envelopes and points toward the graves. "Well, you've told us every detail of their stories, especially Amer's. That counts for something."

"You know, after wartime, it was always such a thrill to see a man come home alive. 'Man alive!' we used to shout when those soldiers got off the train or entered the bar on a Saturday night.

"If only Amer could have . . ."

I remember what the preacher had told my dad and me after we arrived for the funeral all those years ago: the brain and heart handle bad news by increments. They take in whatever they can hold in a moment or a day. Then more thoughts and memories are allowed in as the weeks and months pass.

In an effort to stretch, Nellie staggers backwards in little steps until she can steady herself by gripping the top of the bench.

"Mother and Daddy," she says in a shaky voice, "wondered about Amer's condition. You know, a body traveling such a long distance in that summer heat. Isn't that right, Hannah?"

"Yah, yah. We were surprised at how well he came through. Uncle Vic asked my father to order the very finest metallic casket and a steel grave vault. Our dads took care of that, we'll have you know. As I recall, the funeral was well attended. Wouldn't you say so, Nellie?"

"Oh, yes. The pastor at Aunt Selma's church of worship announced it the Sunday before. So everyone knew about it and could fill the pews."

I make it a point to stand up slowly so as not to teeter about like Nellie.

"After the funeral," I explain, placing Amer's letters into my breast pocket, "Dad and I took the last leg of our journey back to Pipestone, then Hadley and the farm. Mother and Ray were relieved to see us, and happy to have another dog on the place. It didn't take Radge long to make friends with Sport and Docky, and to start scaring up a few birds, especially when we ran together through the cornrows."

"Did you hear his voice echoing over the fields?" asks Cal, her eyes sparkling.

"What's that?"

"You know. Uncle Amer singing and calling out: 'They're taking off on their own now, boys, so just sit back and watch 'em grow!'"

"Oh, yes. Yes, of course." I laugh and give the back of Callie's neck a little squeeze like when she was a girl. "I believe we did, Cal. I do believe we did."

Hannah smiles. "Well, I'd like to know what became of Tom Carmichael."

"He went to trial. Found guilty in the first degree and sentenced to life."

"That's a relief," says Nellie.

"Ah, but he served only two years."

"What?"

Suddenly, I feel as disgusted as I did seven decades ago when we heard that his brothers and father had ponied up enough money to bribe the Judge of District Court.

"That judge arranged for a new trial—this time in Lewiston. As a result, Tom Carmichael was set free, despite witnesses, earlier testimonies, and the fact that Amer's dying declaration could be used as admissible evidence."

"That's awful!" exclaims Nellie.

"Well," says Hannah, "I'm sure the fates eventually took care of Mister Tom Carmichael. That which goes around comes around, don't you know."

"I believe, after some time, he ended up moving away from Jordan, then leaving the state for good on account of the word getting out.

"What about Amer's land?" asks Nellie. "Shouldn't it have gone to our folks?"

"Nope. That acreage went back into the Federal registers. He never got the time needed to prove up on it."

"I can't imagine what we'd do with it, Nellie," says Hannah. "A chunk of land in Eastern Montana? Didn't sound very farmable to me."

"Well, I still say it's a shame." Nellie purses her lips. "Do you think the Carmichaels got it after all?"

"I don't believe so. Of course, we'll never know for sure unless we make an effort to check the records. Anyhow, those Carmichaels are long dead by now."

"Whatever happened to Amer's soddy?"

"I don't know, Nellie. Eventually, I suppose, it crumbled and was plowed back into the earth. Or, maybe someone else took it over."

Thinking about the inside of that 'dobe and the single book I'd left there for someone else to find, tucked away in a darkened corner, its brownish green binding blending with the wooden shelf, I walk slowly back to Amer's unmarked plot here in the cemetery. Yet there was that tiny gleam, wasn't there, coming from the golden lettering on the book's spine: *Leaves of Grass*. And when I had picked it off the shelf to admire the full cover decorated with embossed vines, leaves, and golden roots trailing from the title, the book seemed to open at random, offering up the poem, "Song of Myself." I paused on its third line and read it over again: "For every atom belonging to me as good belongs to you," and then dropped down a few more lines to ". . . The sniff of green leaves and dry leaves, and of the shore and dark-color'd sea-rocks, and of hay in the barn . . ."

I arrive at Amer's ground—that is, the spot where I believe he is buried. Hannah follows, and then stops to wait for Nellie who has sidled up to Cal as if eager to share a secret.

"I didn't want to say this in front of your dad," she whispers, loudly enough for me to hear, "but I think the main reason our folks didn't bother with a tombstone was that they didn't really approve of . . . well, you know . . . how he was and all."

"What do you mean?" Cal looks puzzled.

"Well, you maybe didn't know this about him, but he was always kind of, oh, I don't know. Kind of odd."

"Oh, Nellie," Hannah frowns. "Why don't you just say it. Our uncle was a homosexual."

Isn't the word 'gay'?" asks Nellie.

"Same thing," says Hannah.

My daughter looks stunned, confused, then angry. "And that's why you never bought a tombstone for him?" Her shout makes Nellie take a step backward.

"Well, our folks didn't believe in that sort of thing."

"But he was family, Nellie! Family, for God's sake!"

I stay where I am for a moment, next to the gravesites, proud of my daughter for standing up to this cousin who will never stop parroting her folks. But then I see that Cal is struggling to hold back the tears as her next words tumble out.

"You never knew him. Dad told me all about Uncle Amer. Ever since I was a little kid, I got to know him that way: he played the violin; and he sang Puccini; and he read great books; he had Johnny and Skeeky and a dog named Radge; I read all of his letters; he worked hard for that land; and his soddy? He built that house from dirt.

"He was a somebody!"

I rush over to ally with my daughter and steer her away from the

126

others. Nellie and Hannah head toward the car, talking loudly, gesturing, scowling back at us, perplexed or bewildered; I'm not sure which.

"Why didn't you ever say anything, Dad, that Amer was gay? I mean, I pretty much figured it out from Nellie's earlier innuendos. This is an important part of who he was."

"We're in his corner, Cal. Always have been."

"But why didn't you ever tell me the whole story? That's why the Carmichaels went after him, wasn't it? It wasn't only about the land."

"In those days, we didn't really have a name for men like that. They were just different, that's all. And a place like Montana back then? Or anywhere out west . . ."

"My God, what he must have gone through."

"You were pretty young, Cal, when we first talked about Amer. I told you what I knew for sure, what I thought you could understand at the time."

"I guess you've always done that. Measured things out in little doses until you thought I could handle the big picture."

"Are you criticizing the way your mother and I raised you? You and Liz?"

"No, but didn't the rest of his story seem important enough to tell us? At least, later on? That's why he struggled so. That's why he was murdered. I'll bet the sheriff and the courts used the land dispute as an excuse, a cover-up, and didn't do a damned thing to help him. They just let it happen."

"He was an easy target, Cal. My folks knew it, but they had to let him go. I'm sure you're right. Yet it's hard for me to admit: That his death had more to do with who he was than what he was striving for: some land."

"Which is why the law never protected him, damn their hides!"

"We'll never know any of that for sure—never be able to prove it. As far as I'm concerned, the most important thing was how he lived and struggled to get ahead. He was out there doing the best he could."

With a purpose, Cal walks back to the benches where we'd sat just moments ago and picks a handful of lavender and yellow wildflowers. We return to the graves for a final look at the ground that must belong to Amer. I open my tobacco pouch and sprinkle a fresh handful of the sweet brown flecks onto the grass next to Cal's little bouquet.

She smiles, seems a bit more relaxed. "You learned that up north, didn't you, Dad?"

"Uh-huh."

I recall writing a letter to Cal and Liz about the afternoon I was invited to smoke the peace pipe with a half dozen men from the Leech Lake Band of Ojibwe. During the ceremony, they paid tribute to the four directions, along with Mother Earth, Father sky, and the Great Spirit they call Wakan Tanka. The elder spoke of mankind's responsibilities to others and to the environment. He sprinkled a little tobacco on the ground before placing some in the pipe. "We must give back to Mother Earth a part of what we take," he said.

Another stood up straight, holding his right arm up high, in the direction of the lake and sky. "When a man moves away from nature," he said, "his heart becomes hard."

Then the others spoke and gave colors to the four directions: East is red for the rising sun; South is yellow for the spring bounty; Black stands for the West, after the sun goes down and the spirit world gathers; White stands for the North, where blankets of snow cover the land.

I have always been partial to the East, thanking the Great Spirit for each new day that we're allowed to live upon Mother Earth. Oh, that my uncle had been allowed his full time on this earth.

Suddenly, from across the years, something the pastor had said during Amer's funeral service pops into my head and I recite it for Cal: "An evil act took from us a fine man. Yet his existence added to the collective good of mankind. We must understand that the terrible wrong done to him, the way that he died, makes all the more dear the life that was."

"That's beautiful, Dad. I'm surprised you can remember those exact words after all these years."

"Me, too. They just came to me, though, clear as morning."

"Will you write them down for me?"

"Yes, Callie girl. I'll do that."

My daughter and I walk the rigid, pebbled path back to the car where Hannah and Nellie are waiting in the back seat. Gravel grates against the soles of our shoes, reminding me of the three-day hike we took to Ocheyedan, Iowa, back when Cal was a youngster—one of our many happy times together.

A short distance away, two young boys are playing Hide-and-Seek among the tall headstones. We smile at their laughter and at the dog chasing after them.

Cal hooks her arm through mine. "Maybe we should make another trip back here, Dad. Buy a marker for the grave, something for your grandma and auntie, as well. See that they're all done up right, just as we'd imagined."

"Uh-uh. I don't think so. Not sure that I'll ever be up to coming back."

"Are you sure about that?" she asks, stopping in her tracks. "You were pretty intent on seeing a stone for Amer."

"Well, here's how I need to look at it right now." I spread my arms wide. "He's everywhere. All around us." I circle about in a little soft-shoe (a bit slowly, perhaps) to glance back at the graveyard, at the tall pines and cottonwood branches brushing the sky.

"Every time we see trees like these or a field of corn laid by or a slough filled with chattering ducks or hear a tune by Puccini, there he'll be. Besides, Callie girl, I have a hunch you'll be telling Amer's story long after I'm gone. Now isn't that better than some mossy old stone?"

"Dad," Cal exclaims, looking back at the plots we had examined so closely, "what you just said—that's almost like those lines from *The Grapes of Wrath;* I don't remember the exact words, but they went something like this:

'Whenever there's a fight so hungry people can eat, I'll be there.... Or a cop beating up a guy. . . . I'll be in the way kids laugh . . . when they know supper's ready... An' eat the stuff they raise an' live in the houses they build . . .'"

"I'll be there," I repeat slowly, intent on remembering those words, glad that my daughter knows them. "I have no more regrets, Cal. Your granddad and I did our part bringing Amer home. I'm so glad that he knew he had at least some family members who would always be there for him. Never fail him."

During the silent drive along these October streets, back to Hannah's house, I grip the steering wheel and picture my uncle's unlabored movements in the fields, his gentle way with the livestock, his thin, yet muscular white legs in rolled up overalls.

And then I go back to that one summer afternoon. The sun is hot. We are all lounging together on a grassy slope at the edge of Lake Summit—my father and mother, my brother and our dogs, my uncle and I.

And Uncle Amer is singing a song that would like to make you cry.